Tom's Midnight Garden

8379

Author PEARCE F.

Title Tom's MID

A. PHILIPPA PEARCE

TOM'S
MIDNIGHT
GARDEN

Illustrated by
Susan Einzig

London
OXFORD UNIVERSITY
PRESS

Oxford University Press, Amen House, London E.C.4

GLASGOW NEW YORK TORONTO MELBOURNE WELLINGTON
BOMBAY CALCUTTA MADRAS KARACHI LAHORE DACCA
CAPE TOWN SALISBURY NAIROBI IBADAN ACCRA
KUALA LUMPUR HONG KONG

First edition 1958
Reprinted 1959, 1962

Awarded the Library Association's Carnegie
Medal for an outstanding children's book of
1958

Printed in Great Britain by Richard Clay and Company, Ltd.,
Bungay, Suffolk

CONTENTS

I

Exile

IF, standing alone on the back doorstep, Tom allowed himself to weep tears, they were tears of anger. He looked his good-bye at the garden, and raged that he had to leave it—leave it and Peter. They had planned to spend their time here so joyously these holidays.

Town gardens are small, as a rule, and the Longs' garden was no exception to the rule; there was a vegetable plot and a grass plot and one flower-bed and a rough patch by the back fence. In this last the apple-tree grew: it was large, but bore very little fruit, and accordingly the two boys had always been allowed to climb freely over it.

These holidays they would have built a tree-house among its branches.

Tom gazed, and then turned back into the house. As he passed the foot of the stairs, he called up, 'Good-bye, Peter!' There was a croaking answer.

He went out on to the front doorstep, where his mother was waiting with his suitcase. He put his hand out for it, but Mrs Long clung to the case for a moment, claiming his attention first. 'You know, Tom,' she said, 'it's not nice for you to be rushed away like this to avoid the measles, but it's not nice for us either. Your father and I will miss you, and so will Peter. Peter's not having a nice time, anyway, with measles.'

'I didn't say you'd all be having a nice time without me,' said Tom. 'All I said was——'

'Hush!' whispered his mother, looking past him to the road and the car that waited there and the man at its driving-wheel. She gave Tom the case, and then bent over him, pushing his tie up to cover his collar-button and letting her lips come to within a few inches of his ear. 'Tom, dear Tom——' she murmured, trying to prepare him for the weeks ahead, 'remember that you will be a visitor, and do try—oh, what can I say?—try to be *good*.'

She kissed him, gave him a dismissive push towards the car and then followed him to it. As Tom got in, Mrs Long looked past him to the driver. 'Give my love to Gwen,' she said, 'and tell her, Alan, how grateful we are to you both for taking Tom off at such short notice. It's very kind of you, isn't it, Tom?'

'Very kind,' Tom repeated bitterly.

'There's so little room in the house,' said Mrs Long, 'when there's illness.'

'We're glad to help out,' Alan said. He started the engine.

Tom wound down the window next to his mother. 'Good-bye then!'

'Oh, Tom!' Her lips trembled. 'I am sorry—spoiling the beginning of your summer holidays like this!'

The car was moving; he had to shout back: 'I'd rather have had measles with Peter—much rather!'

Tom waved good-bye angrily to his mother, and then, careless even of the cost to others, waved to an inflamed face pressed against a bedroom window. Mrs Long looked upwards to see what was there, raised her hands in a gesture of despair—Peter was supposed to keep strictly to his bed—and hurried indoors.

Tom closed the car window and sat back in his seat, in hostile silence. His uncle cleared his throat and said: 'Well, I hope we get on reasonably well.'

This was not a question, so Tom did not answer it.

He knew he was being rude, but he made excuses for himself: he did not much like Uncle Alan, and he did not want to like him at all. Indeed, he would have preferred him to be a brutal uncle. 'If only he'd beat me,' thought Tom, 'then I could run away home, and Mother and Father would say I did right, in spite of the quarantine for measles. But he'll never even try to beat me, I know; and Aunt Gwen—she's worse, because she's a child-lover, and she's kind. Cooped up for weeks with Uncle Alan and Aunt Gwen in a poky flat . . .' He had never visited them before, but he knew that they lived in a flat, with no garden.

They drove in silence. Their route took them through Ely; but they only stopped for Alan Kitson to buy a picture-postcard of the cathedral tower. It was for Tom. Tom was bitterly disappointed that he was not allowed to climb the tower, but his uncle pointed out to him with great reasonableness that this was quite out of the question: he was in quarantine for measles. He must not mix with Peter, in case he caught his measles; and he must not mix with other people either, in case he already *had* Peter's measles. Fortunately, the Kitsons had both had measles, anyway.

They drove on through Ely and the Fens, and then through Castleford and beyond, to where the Kitsons lived, in a big house now converted into flats. The house was crowded round with newer, smaller houses that beat up to its very confines in a broken sea of bay-windows and gable-ends and pinnacles. It was the only big house among them: oblong, plain, grave.

Alan Kitson sounded the car-horn and turned into the drive—only it was really too short to be called a drive now. 'The house had a better frontage, I believe, until they built up opposite, and had to widen the road too.' He pulled up outside a pillared front-door; and Aunt Gwen appeared in the doorway, laughing and wanting to kiss Tom. She drew him inside, and Uncle Alan followed with the luggage.

There were cold stone flags under Tom's feet, and in his nostrils a smell of old dust that it had been nobody's business to disperse. As he looked round, he felt a chill. The hall of the big house was not mean nor was it ugly, but it was unwelcoming. Here it lay at the heart of the house— for it went centrally from front to back with a sideways part to the stair-foot, in a T-shape—and the heart of the house was empty—cold—dead. Someone had pinned bright travel-posters on to the high, grey walls; someone had left a laundry-box with its laundry-list, in a corner; there were empty milk-bottles against a far door, with a message to the milkman: none of these things seemed really to belong to the hall. It remained empty and silent —silent unless one counted the voice of Aunt Gwen chattering on about Tom's mother and Peter's measles. When her voice died for a moment, Tom heard the only sound that went on: the tick, and then tick, and then tick, of a grandfather clock.

'No, don't touch it, Tom,' said Aunt Gwen, as he turned towards it. She lowered her voice. 'It belongs to old Mrs Bartholomew upstairs, and she's rather particular about it.'

Tom had never looked inside a grandfather clock, and he thought it might be something to do later, privately: surely, he could just look. Now, with his back to the clock, innocently continuing to converse with his aunt, he slipped his finger-nails under the edge of the door of the pendulum-case, to try it . . .

'If Mrs Bartholomew's particular about her clock, why doesn't she have it upstairs with her?' Tom asked. He levered gently with his nails: the door was resisting him . . .

'Because the clock is screwed to the wall at the back, and

the screws have rusted in,' said Aunt Gwen. 'Come away from it, do, Tom. Come up to tea.'

'Oh!' said Tom, as if he had not realized where he was standing. He moved away. The pendulum door had been locked.

They were going upstairs to the Kitsons' flat when, from behind them, the grandfather clock struck one, with stately emphasis. Uncle Alan frowned and made some cutting comment. The clock kept good time—its fingers were now correctly pointing to five o'clock—but it seldom chose to strike the right hour. It was utterly unreliable in its striking, Uncle Alan said. Moreover, the voice of the clock was so penetrating that he could even hear it being unreliable when he was upstairs in bed, at night.

They had reached the first floor, where the Kitsons lived. Beyond, another, narrow staircase mounted to the attic flat of Mrs Bartholomew, who owned the grandfather clock and, indeed, the whole house. She was the landlady, and the Kitsons—like the other inhabitants of the big house—were her tenants.

'This is our flat, Tom dear,' said Aunt Gwen; 'and here is the guest-room—your bedroom. I've put flowers in it, and books for you to read.' She smiled at him, begging him with her eyes to like staying here.

Tom's bedroom was lofty, but otherwise only of medium size. There was another door in it, like the door of entry. The window—large and large-paned—was one of those he had seen from outside. Tom had been preparing himself to play the grateful guest; but——

'But there are bars across the bottom of the window!' he burst out. 'This is a nursery! I'm not a baby!'

'Of course not—of course not!' Aunt Gwen cried, equally upset. 'It's nothing to do with you, Tom. This window had bars across it when we came. The bathroom window had too, for that matter.'

Tom's suspicions were not entirely stilled.

When he was left to unpack, before tea, Tom examined the room more closely. The other door only led into a cupboard for clothes; the books were school stories for girls, from Aunt Gwen's own childhood; and there, above all—however much Aunt Gwen tried to explain them away—were the nursery bars to the window.

However, tea cheered Tom a little. Aunt Gwen had made a Devonshire tea, with boiled eggs, home-made scones and home-made strawberry jam and whipped cream. She was a good cook, she said, and she enjoyed cooking; she intended to spoil Tom for food while he was with them.

After tea, Tom wrote a letter of safe arrival to his mother. He enclosed a picture-postcard for Peter, with a very fair statement of his situation. 'I hope your measles are better,' he wrote. 'This is a picture of the cathedral tower at Ely.' (Tom knew that Peter would be interested: the two of them made a point of climbing church towers, as well as trees.) 'We came through Ely, but U.A. wouldn't let me go up the tower. The house here is flats and there isn't any garden. My bedroom window has bars, but A.G. says it's a mistake. The food is good.'

After reading this through, Tom decided—in fairness to

Aunt Gwen—to underline the last sentence. He signed the postcard with his private device: an elongated cat, supposed to be a tom. It signified Tom Long.

He was marking in the whiskers of the cat, when he heard the sound of the grandfather clock from below in the hall. Yes, you could hear it striking, very distinctly; you could count the strokes. Tom counted them, and smiled condescendingly: the clock was wrong again in its striking —senselessly wrong.

II

The Clock Strikes Thirteen

THE striking of the grandfather clock became a familiar sound to Tom, especially in the silence of those nights when everyone else was asleep. He did not sleep. He would go to bed at the usual time, and then lie awake or half-awake for hour after hour. He had never suffered from sleeplessness before in his life, and wondered at it now; but a certain tightness and unease in his stomach should have given him an answer. Sometimes he would doze, and then, in his half-dreaming, he became two persons, and one of him would not go to sleep but selfishly insisted on keeping the other awake with a little muttering monologue on whipped cream and shrimp sauce and rum butter and real mayonnaise and all the other rich variety of his diet nowadays. From that Tom was positively relieved to wake up again.

Aunt Gwen's cooking was the cause of Tom's sleeplessness—that and lack of exercise. Tom had to stay indoors and do crossword puzzles and jigsaw puzzles, and never even answered the door when the milkman came, in case he gave the poor man measles. The only exercise he took was in the kitchen when he was helping his aunt to cook those large, rich meals—larger and richer than Tom had ever known before.

Tom had few ideas on the causes and cures of sleeplessness, and it never occurred to him to complain. At first he tried to read himself to sleep with Aunt Gwen's schoolgirl stories. They did not even bore him enough for that; but he persevered with them. Then Uncle Alan had found him still reading at half-past eleven at night. There had been an outcry. After that Tom was rationed to ten minutes reading in bed; and he had to promise not to switch the bedroom light on again after it had been switched off and his aunt had bidden him good night. He did not regret the reading, but the dragging hours seemed even longer in the dark.

One night he had been lying awake as usual, fretting against the dark and against the knowledge that his uncle and aunt would be sitting reading—talking—doing whatever they pleased—by the excellent electric lights of the sitting-room. Here *he* was, wide awake in the dark with nothing to do. He had borne it for what seemed many nights, but suddenly, tonight, he could bear it no more. He sat up, threw his bedclothes back with a masterful gesture, and stepped out of bed, though as yet with no clear purpose. He felt his way over to the bedroom door, opened it quietly and passed out into the tiny hall of the flat.

Tom could hear the sound of the ordered speaking of Uncle Alan, from behind the sitting-room door: he would be reading aloud from his favourite, clever weekly newspaper; Aunt Gwen would be devotedly listening, or asleep.

A moment's thought, and Tom had glided into the kitchen and thence into the larder. This would have been a routine move at home; he and Peter had often done it.

In Aunt Gwen's larder there were two cold pork chops, half a trifle, some bananas and some buns and cakes. Tom tried to persuade himself that he hesitated only because he didn't know which to choose, but he knew that he was not hungry. As a matter of form, he laid hold of a very plain, stale bun. Then, a great weariness of all food overcame him, and he put the bun down, leaving it to another day of existence.

He had been moving all this time in perfect silence—he would have been ashamed for his skill in such an expedition to have done otherwise. But he had ill-luck: as he went out from the kitchen and larder, he came face to face with his uncle coming from the sitting-room. His uncle's

B

exclamation of surprise and disapproval brought his aunt out after him.

Tom knew that he was in the wrong, of course, but they need not have made such a fuss. Aunt Gwen was most upset because, if Tom slipped into the larder at night, that meant he was hungry. She was not feeding him properly. He was suffering from night starvation.

Uncle Alan, on the other hand, had not been unobservant of Tom at mealtimes, and he could not credit his being hungry. Besides, Tom had admitted he took nothing from the larder. Why had he been there, then? Was it a blind? What *was* it?

Tom never really convinced them of the simple truth: that a boy would naturally go into the larder, even if he were not hungry. Anyway, they pointed out, he was out of bed far too late. He was hustled back again, and his uncle stood over him to make a speech.

'Tom, there must be no more of this. You are not to put the light on again once it has been put out; nor, equally, are you to get out of bed. You must see the reasonableness——'

'Not even to get up in the morning?' Tom interrupted.

'Of course, that's different. Don't be silly, Tom. But you are not to get up otherwise. The reason is——'

'Can't I get up, even if I need to, badly?'

'Of course you must go to the lavatory, if you need to; but you will go straight back to bed afterwards. You go to bed at nine in the evening and get up at seven in the morning. That is ten hours. You need those ten hours' sleep because——'

'But, Uncle Alan, I don't sleep!'

'Will you be quiet, Tom!' shouted his uncle, suddenly losing his temper. 'I'm trying to reason with you! Now, where was I?'

'Ten hours' sleep,' said Tom subduedly.

'Yes, a child of your age needs ten hours of sleep. You must realize that, Tom. For that reason, you must be in bed for ten hours, as I have said. I am making clear to you, Tom, that Gwen and I wish you, entirely for your own good, to be in bed and, if possible, asleep for ten hours, as near as maybe, from nine o'clock at night. You understand, Tom?'

'Yes.'

'Now I want you to promise to observe our wishes. Will you promise, Tom?'

Why could a boy never refuse to promise these large demands? 'I suppose so,' said Tom. 'Yes.'

'There!' said Aunt Gwen; and Uncle Alan said: 'Good. I knew I could reason with you.'

'But, all the same, I don't sleep!'

Uncle Alan said sharply, 'All children sleep;' and Aunt Gwen added more gently: 'It's just your imagination, Tom.'

Poor Tom had no answer except contradiction, and he felt that would be unwise.

They left him.

He lay in the dark, planning a letter to his mother. 'Take me away. At once.' But no, that was perhaps cowardly, and would worry his mother dreadfully. He would unburden himself to Peter instead, although Peter,

because of his measles, could not reply. He would tell
Peter how miserably dull it was here, even at night: nothing to do, nowhere to go, nobody—to speak of—to do
things with. 'It's the worst hole I've ever been in,' he
wrote, in imagination. 'I'd do anything to get out of it,
Peter—to be somewhere else—anywhere.' It seemed to
him that his longing to be free swelled up in him and in
the room, until it should surely be large enough to burst
the walls and set him free indeed.

They had left him, and now they were going to bed.
Uncle Alan took a bath, and Tom lay listening to him and
hating him. For some reason, Tom could always hear
what went on in the bathroom next door to his bedroom as
clearly as if he were there himself: tonight he was almost
in the bath with Uncle Alan. Later he heard other movements and conversation from elsewhere in the flat. Finally,
the line of light under his door disappeared: that meant that
the hall-light of the flat had been switched off for the night.

Slow silence, and then the grandfather clock struck for
twelve. By midnight his uncle and aunt were always in
bed, and asleep too, usually. Only Tom lay still open-
eyed and sullen, imprisoned in wakefulness.

And at last—One! The clock struck the present hour;
but, as if to show its independence of mind, went on striking—Two! For once Tom was not amused by its striking
the wrong hour: Three! Four! 'It's one o'clock,' Tom
whispered angrily over the edge of the bedclothes. 'Why
don't you strike one o'clock, then, as the clocks would do
at home?' Instead: Five! Six! Even in his irritation, Tom
could not stop counting; it had become a habit with him

at night. Seven! Eight! After all, the clock was the only thing that would speak to him at all in these hours of darkness. Nine! Ten! 'You are going it,' thought Tom, but yawning in the midst of his unwilling admiration. Yes, and it hadn't finished yet: Eleven! Twelve! 'Fancy striking midnight twice in one night!' jeered Tom, sleepily. Thirteen! proclaimed the clock, and then stopped striking.

Thirteen? Tom's mind gave a jerk: had it really struck thirteen? Even mad old clocks never struck that. He must have imagined it. Had he not been falling asleep, or already sleeping? But no, awake or dozing, he had counted up to thirteen. He was sure of it.

He was uneasy in the knowledge that this happening made some difference to him: he could feel that in his bones. The stillness had become an expectant one; the house seemed to hold its breath; the darkness pressed up to him, pressing him with a question: Come on, Tom, the clock has struck thirteen—what are you going to do about it?

'Nothing,' said Tom aloud. And then, as an afterthought: 'Don't be silly!'

What *could* he do, anyway? He had to stay in bed, sleeping or trying to sleep, for ten whole hours, as near as might be, from nine o'clock at night to seven o'clock the next morning. That was what he had promised when his uncle had reasoned with him.

Uncle Alan had been so sure of his reasoning; and yet Tom now began to feel that there had been some flaw in it . . . Uncle Alan, without discussing the idea, had taken for granted that there were twenty-four hours in a day—

twice twelve hours. But suppose, instead, there were twice thirteen? Then, from nine at night to seven in the morning—with the thirteenth hour somewhere between —was more than ten hours: it was eleven. He could be in bed for ten hours, and still have an hour to spare—an hour of freedom.

But steady, steady! This was ridiculous: there simply were not thirteen hours in a half day, everyone knew that. But why had the clock said there were, then? You couldn't get round that. Yes, but everyone knew the grandfather clock struck the hours at the wrong times of day—one o'clock when it was really five, and so on. Admittedly, argued the other Tom—the one that would never let the sleepy Tom go to sleep—admittedly the clock struck the hours at the wrong time; but, all the same, they *were* hours —real hours—hours that really existed. Now the clock had struck thirteen, affirming that—for this once at least— there was an extra, thirteenth hour.

'But it just can't be true,' said Tom aloud. The house, which appeared to have been following the argument, sighed impatiently. 'At least, I think it isn't true; and any- way it's muddling.' Meanwhile you're missing your chance, whispered the house. 'I can't honourably take it,' said Tom, 'because I don't believe the grandfather clock was telling the truth when it struck thirteen.' Oh, said the house coldly, so it's a liar, is it?

Tom sat up in bed, a little angry in his turn. 'Now,' he said, 'I'm going to prove this, one way or the other. I'm going to see what the clock fingers say. I'm going down to the hall.'

III

By Moonlight

THIS was a real expedition. Tom put on his bedroom slippers, but decided against his dressing-gown: after all, it was summer. He closed his bedroom door carefully behind him, so that it should not bang in his absence. Outside the front door of the flat he took off one of his slippers; he laid it on the floor against the door jamb and then closed the door on to it, as on to a wedge. That would keep the door open for his return.

The lights on the first-floor landing and in the hall were turned out, for the tenants were all in bed and asleep, and Mrs Bartholomew was asleep and dreaming. The only illumination was a sideways shaft of moonlight through the long window part way up the stairs. Tom felt his way downstairs and into the hall.

Here he was checked. He could find the grandfather clock—a tall and ancient figure of black in the lesser blackness—but he was unable to read its face. If he opened its dial-door and felt until he found the position of the clock-hands, then his sense of touch would tell him the time. He fumbled first at one side of the door, then at the other; but there seemed no catch—no way in. He remembered how the pendulum-case door had not yielded to him either, on that first day. Both must be kept locked.

Hurry! hurry! the house seemed to whisper round him. The hour is passing . . . passing . . .

Tom turned from the clock to feel for the electric-light switch. Where had it been? His fingers swept the walls in vain: nowhere.

Light—light: that was what he needed! And the only light was the moonbeam that glanced sideways through the stairway window and spent itself at once and uselessly on the wall by the window-sill.

Tom studied the moonbeam, with an idea growing in his mind. From the direction in which the beam came, he saw that the moon must be shining at the back of the house. Very well, then, if he opened the door at the far end of the hall—at the back of the house, that is—he would let that moonlight in. With luck there might be enough light for him to read the clock-face.

He moved down the hall to the door at its far end. It was a door he had never seen opened—the Kitsons used the door at the front. They said that the door at the back was only a less convenient way to the street, through a back-yard—a strip of paving where dustbins were kept and where the tenants of the ground-floor back flat garaged their car under a tarpaulin.

Never having had occasion to use the door, Tom had no idea how it might be secured at night. If it were locked, and the key kept elsewhere . . . But it was not locked, he found; only bolted. He drew the bolt and, very slowly, to make no sound, turned the door-knob.

Hurry! whispered the house; and the grandfather clock at the heart of it beat an anxious tick, tick.

Tom opened the door wide and let in the moonlight. It flooded in, as bright as daylight—the white daylight that comes before the full rising of the sun. The illumination was perfect, but Tom did not at once turn to see what it showed him of the clock-face. Instead he took a step forward on to the doorstep. He was staring, at first in surprise, then with indignation, at what he saw outside. That they should have deceived him—lied to him—like this! They had said, 'It's not worth your while going out at the back, Tom.' So carelessly they had described it: 'A sort of back-yard, very poky, with rubbish bins. Really, there's nothing to see.'

Nothing . . . Only this: a great lawn where flower-beds bloomed; a towering fir-tree, and thick, beetle-browed yews that humped their shapes down two sides of the lawn; on the third side, to the right, a greenhouse almost the size of a real house; from each corner of the lawn, a path that twisted away to some other depths of garden, with other trees.

Tom had stepped forward instinctively, catching his breath in surprise; now he let his breath out in a deep sigh. He would steal out here tomorrow, by daylight. They had tried to keep this from him, but they could not stop him now—not his aunt, nor his uncle, nor the back flat tenants, nor even particular Mrs Bartholomew. He would run full tilt over the grass, leaping the flower-beds; he would peer through the glittering panes of the greenhouse—perhaps open the door and go in; he would visit each alcove and archway clipped in the yew-trees—he would climb the trees and make his way from one to another through thickly interlacing branches. When they came calling him, he would hide, silent and safe as a bird, among this richness of leaf and bough and tree-trunk.

The scene tempted him even now: it lay so inviting and clear before him—clear-cut from the stubby leaf-pins of the nearer yew-trees to the curled-back petals of the hyacinths in the crescent-shaped corner beds. Yet Tom remembered his ten hours and his honour. Regretfully he turned from the garden, back indoors to read the grandfather clock.

He re-crossed the threshold, still absorbed in the thought of what he had seen outside. For that reason, perhaps, he could not at once make out how the hall had become different: his eyes informed him of some shadowy change; his bare foot was trying to tell him something . . . *what?*

The grandfather clock was still there, anyway, and must tell him the true time. It must be either twelve or one: there was no hour between. There is no thirteenth hour.

Tom never reached the clock with his inquiry, and may be excused for forgetting, on this occasion, to check its truthfulness. His attention was distracted by the opening of a door down the hall—the door of the ground-floor front flat. A maid trotted out.

Tom had seen housemaids only in pictures, but he recognized the white apron, cap and cuffs, and the black stockings. (He was not expert in fashions, but the dress seemed to him to be rather long for her.) She was carrying paper, kindling wood and a box of matches.

He had only a second in which to observe these things. Then he realized that he ought to take cover at once; and there was no cover to take. Since he must be seen, Tom determined to be the first to speak—to explain himself.

He did not feel afraid of the maid: as she came nearer, he saw that she was only a girl. To warn her of his presence without startling her, Tom gave a cough; but she did not seem to hear it. She came on. Tom moved forward into her line of vision; she looked at him, but looked through him, too, as though he were not there. Tom's heart jumped in a way he did not understand. She was passing him. *Why?*

'I say!' he protested loudly; but she paid not the slightest attention. She passed him, reached the front door of the ground-floor back flat, turned the door-handle and went in. There was no bell-ringing or unlocking of the door.

Tom was left gaping; and, meanwhile, his senses began to insist upon telling him of experiences even stranger than this encounter. His one bare foot was on cold flagstone, he knew; yet there was a contradictory softness and warmth to this flagstone. He looked down and saw that he was standing on a rug—a tiger-skin rug. There were other rugs down the hall. His eyes now took in the whole of the hall—a hall that was different. No laundry box, no milk bottles, no travel posters on the walls. The walls were decorated with a rich variety of other objects instead: a tall Gothic barometer, a fan of peacock feathers, a huge engraving of a battle (hussars and horses and shot-riddled banners) and many other pictures. There was a big dinner gong, with its wash-leathered gong-stick hanging beside it. There was a large umbrella stand holding umbrellas and walking-sticks and a parasol and an air-gun and what looked like the parts of a fishing-rod. Along the wall projected a series of bracket-shelves, each table-high. They were of oak, except for one towards the middle of the hall, by the grandfather clock. That was of white marble, and it was piled high with glass cases of stuffed birds and animals. Enacted on its chilly surface were scenes of hot bloodshed: an owl clutched a mouse in its claws; a ferret looked up from the killing of its rabbit; in a case in the middle a red fox slunk along with a gamefowl hanging from its jaws.

In all that crowded hall, the only object that Tom recognized was the grandfather clock. He moved towards it, not to read its face, but simply to touch it—to reassure himself that this at least was as he knew it.

His hand was nearly upon it, when he heard a little breath behind him that was the maid passing back the way she had come. For some reason, she did not seem to make as much sound as before. He heard her call only faintly: 'I've lit the fire in the parlour.'

She was making for the door through which she had first come, and, as Tom followed her with his eyes, he received a curious impression: she reached the door, her hand was upon the knob, and then she seemed to go. That was it exactly: she went, but not through the door. She simply thinned out, and went.

Even as he stared at where she had been, Tom became aware of something going on furtively and silently about him. He looked round sharply, and caught the hall in the act of emptying itself of furniture and rugs and pictures. They were not positively going, perhaps, but rather beginning to fail to be there. The Gothic barometer, for instance, was there, before he turned to look at the red fox; when he turned back, the barometer was still there, but it had the appearance of something only sketched against the wall, and the wall was visible through it; meanwhile the fox had slunk into nothingness, and all the other creatures were going with him; and, turning back again swiftly to the barometer, Tom found that gone already.

In a matter of seconds the whole hall was as he had seen it on his first arrival. He stood dumbfounded. He was roused from his stupefaction by the chill of a draught at his back: it reminded him that the garden door was left open.

Whatever else had happened, he had really opened that door; and he must shut it. He must go back to bed.

He closed the door after a long look: 'I shall come back,' he promised silently to the trees and the lawn and the green-house.

Upstairs, again, in bed, he pondered more calmly on what he had seen in the hall. Had it been a dream? Another possible explanation occurred to him: ghosts. That was what they could all have been: ghosts. The hall was haunted by the ghost of a housemaid and a barometer and a stuffed fox and a stuffed owl and by the ghosts of dozens of other things. Indeed, if it were haunted at all, the hall was overhaunted.

Ghosts . . . Tom doubtfully put his hand up out of the bedclothes to see if his hair were standing on end. It was not. Nor, he remembered, had he felt any icy chill when the maid had looked at him and through him.

He was dissatisfied with his own explanation, and suddenly sick of needing to explain at all. It was not as if the hall were of great interest, with or without a maid and all the rest; the garden was the thing. That was real. To-morrow he would go into it: he almost had the feel of tree-trunks between his hands as he climbed; he could almost smell the heavy blooming of the hyacinths in the corner beds. He remembered that smell from home: in-doors, from his mother's bulb pots, at Christmas and the New Year; outside, in their flower-bed, in the late spring. He fell asleep thinking of home.

IV

By Daylight

THE next morning, when Tom woke, he could not think why he felt so happy, until he remembered the garden. The appearances in the hall seemed less likely than ever; but the impression on his mind of what he had seen through the garden door remained unchanged. Yet now he began to think that visiting the garden would be less easy than he had reckoned last night. His aunt and uncle would certainly do all they could to stop him; they did not want him to use the garden, else why had they kept him in the dark about its very existence?

That made Tom remember his anger against them, and he determined to shame them. He would have to play a very careful game: by innocent-seeming references he must hit home, without ever letting them suspect that he knew of the garden and intended to go there.

He began at breakfast.

'Do you believe that lying is wrong?'

'Oh, Tom!' cried Aunt Gwen. 'Always!'

'I mean,' said Tom, 'do you think that some special lies might be right, sometimes?'

'Is lying ever justifiable?' This was the kind of question Uncle Alan liked to discuss. He folded away his paper and cleared his throat. 'I suppose, Tom, you are thinking of what are commonly known as white lies?'

'I don't think so, exactly,' said Tom. 'At least, I mean —well, someone being kept in the dark about something he'd enjoy, because some other people didn't want to tell him about it. I mean, supposing the other people went so far as to say the thing just wasn't there, in order not to have the bother of the first person using it.'

Aunt Gwen looked confused. 'What kind of thing was it the second people didn't want the first people to know about and use?'

'First person, not first people,' said Tom. 'And the thing was—well——'

'A hot-water bottle, say?' suggested Aunt Gwen.

'No,' said Tom, 'more like'—he tried to think of something between a hot-water bottle and a large garden— 'more like a couch, say—a large *outdoor* couch.'

'I'm not sure that I've ever heard of such a thing,' said Aunt Gwen. 'A large outdoor couch?'

'It doesn't really matter what the thing is, Gwen,' said Uncle Alan impatiently. 'If I understand Tom, the point is that some person or persons were lying simply for their own convenience, and to the harm of another person or persons. Is that so, Tom?'

'Yes,' said Tom. 'I just wondered if you thought that kind of lie might be right. I just wondered.'

'Of all possible forms of lying,' said Uncle Alan, 'that is surely the least justifiable. Indeed, it is utterly and obviously unjustifiable.' He looked severely at Tom. 'I am surprised, Tom, that you should have any doubts about it.' He gathered his newspaper and post together and went off to work.

'Never mind, Tom,' said Aunt Gwen. 'Uncle Alan has a very highly developed sense of right and wrong. He says so himself. You will have one too, I'm sure, when you grow up.'

'I have one now!' said Tom indignantly. 'It's other people who haven't!'

Tom had not intended to harry Aunt Gwen apart from Uncle Alan: that had seemed unsportsmanlike. Generous resolutions, however, often break down under the strain of nothing more serious than annoyance, and Tom was now very much annoyed. He had been made to feel in the wrong, when he was in the right; and the people who had made him feel that were themselves the wrongdoers.

Tom helped to clear the breakfast-table and followed his aunt to the sink. He began to dry up, darkly intent.

'Aunt Gwen.'

'Yes, Tom?'

'It was kind of you to put flowers in my bedroom when I came.'

c

'Tom, dear, I didn't know you'd noticed them!'

'Had you to buy them?'

'Yes, but you mustn't bother about that.'

'It would have been easier for you if you'd been able to get flowers from a garden of your own.'

'Yes, but there isn't a garden to this house, of course.'

'No?'

'What do you mean by "No", Tom?'

'I meant, What a pity! Wouldn't it be nice if there were a garden at the back of the house—with a lawn and trees and flowers and even a greenhouse?'

'It would be nice, too, if we had wings and could fly, Tom.'

'Suppose you could walk out of the door at the back this very minute, Aunt Gwen—this very minute—and walk on to a lawn and cut hyacinths from the flower-beds on that lawn—from little corner beds shaped like the quarters of an orange—what would you say, Aunt Gwen? What do you say now?'

He had as good as told her that he knew all about the garden; he had challenged her openly.

Aunt Gwen did not start or show shame; she laughed. 'To begin with, Tom, I should be very surprised indeed if you picked me a hyacinth from anywhere outside, now.'

'Oh?'

'Hyacinths don't flower even out of doors at this time of year—it's too late in the summer. See what your romancing has led you into!'

'But I've s-*seen* hyacinths flowering out of doors, at just this time of year,' said Tom. He stammered because he was frightened.

'No, Tom, you can't have. They're quite over.'

Tom put down the plate he had been drying—it was still damp—and the tea-cloth. 'I'm going downstairs, if you don't mind.'

'What for, Tom?'

'Nothing special. I won't do anything wrong.'

'Don't go this morning. This is the morning that Mrs Bartholomew always goes downstairs to wind the grandfather clock.'

His aunt's warning only sped Tom: he told himself that she was inventing an excuse to keep him from the garden. He was still afraid, all the same—and not of Mrs Bartholomew.

As he ran down the stairs to the hall, Tom was remembering the hyacinths: he had seen the curling back of the petals; he had smelt them. They had been real last night; they were real now. He had only to open the garden door to see them again—to see the whole of his garden again.

He reached the garden door and turned its handle; but the door was fastened. He found the bolt, as he had done last night, but it was already drawn; and the bolt had a granular roughness to the touch that he recognized as rust—more rust than could have been formed in one night. Tom tried to move the bolt in its socket, but it was rusted up completely. It had been rusted up, one could tell, for years.

The door was fastened now by an ordinary, modern Yale lock. Tom turned its little knob, but hesitated to open the door. He felt a sickness in his stomach, as though he had eaten the wrong things at breakfast: perhaps he ought to go straight back upstairs to bed. Besides, his head was swimming a little, and he felt a chill over his skin.

Suddenly he cried aloud angrily: 'Don't be a fool! It's there, I tell you! The garden's there!' He flung the door wide open, and blinked into the morning sunlight.

At the back of the house was a narrow, paved space enclosed by a wooden fence, with a gateway on to the side-road at one end. There were five dustbins, and near the dustbins was parked an old car from beneath which stuck a pair of legs in trousers. A piece of newspaper bowled about, blown in from outside and imprisoned here; and the place smelt of sun on stone and metal and the creosote of the fencing.

The man under the car crawled out at the sound of the door's opening. He had a short ginger beard; otherwise there was nothing whatsoever of interest about him.

'Hallo!' he said. 'Who are you?'

Tom did not answer.

'Oh, I know—you're the boy from the first-floor front —the Kitsons'. A bit dull for you here, isn't it?'

'Yes,' said Tom. 'Do you live in the ground-floor back flat?'

'Yes,' said ginger beard. He looked at Tom curiously: the boy's voice sounded strange.

'Do you have a maid that lights your fire for you?'

'A *what*?'

'And you don't—you don't have a garden either?

To ginger beard's amazement, the boy on the doorstep,

without waiting for an answer to his last question, burst into tears.

'Here, I say! What on earth's the matter?'

'Leave me alone!' Tom turned to stumble indoors again.

'Wait—wait a minute!' There was something imperative in the man's voice. 'Listen!' Tom halted, and held back his desolate crying. 'I thought so,' said the man softly.

In the quiet, they could hear, from indoors, the ticking of the grandfather clock, and the sound of someone shuffling down the stairs.

'It's old Ma Bartholomew,' whispered ginger beard. 'Coming to wind up her precious clock. You don't want to run into her. There've never been children here, and she might not like it.'

Tom drew back out of sight into the doorway. His arm was still up to his face to hide the tears, but his eyes now looked over the top.

The shuffling steps came nearer; the figure of Mrs Bartholomew appeared. She was old, small and bowed; she was dressed all in black.

When she reached the clock, Mrs Bartholomew took from her purse a key, and opened the door of the pendulum case with it. She reached inside the case and brought out something small and polished that looked like the starting-handle of some tiny car. She reached up inside the case again, and must have pressed a lever that latched the glass front of the clock-dial: the front swung open at her touch.

She took what had looked like a miniature starting-handle and fitted it into a slot on the right-hand side of the dial, and turned and turned it. As she wound, there was a gentle whirring sound. Then she wound on the other side of the dial.

Finally, she latched the dial-front again, put the winding-key back inside the pendulum-case, locked the case-door, and shuffled away with the key. Her footsteps climbed the stairs and died away.

While he was watching the clock being wound, Tom had had time to calm himself. He began to reason about the garden. It was true that there was no garden this morning, but there certainly had been last night—hyacinths and all. He turned back to look again at what was outside, searching for some link between last night and this morning. Up to the fence of the back-yard ran strips of garden that belonged to the pink brick, semi-detached houses beyond. In one of the garden strips stood an old yew-tree. Once, certainly, the tree had been clipped to a shape.

Tom stared at it with a kind of hope.

'What's bitten you now?' said the man.

'Nothing,' said Tom. 'Thank you for warning me about Mrs Bartholomew. Good-bye.'

He went slowly down the hall, thinking. The tree was perhaps a link; but it was out of his reach, in another garden. The big house itself was a link, of course; but it would tell him nothing. He had already taken the turn to the stairway when the voice of the grandfather clock behind him reminded him: the clock was a link.

He went back to the grandfather clock and studied it

intently. The clock-case was plain. The dial bore only twelve numbers, after all; but it was decorated with a design that now struck Tom as peculiar and interesting. In the semicircular arch above the dial itself stood a creature like a man but with enormous, sweeping wings. His body was wound about with something white. His face was a round of gold, and his feet were of the same colour and were planted on either side of the clock-dial. One foot seemed to stand on a piece of grassy land: the other went into the sea—Tom saw painted fishes that swam round the creature's foot, and seaweed. In one hand he held a book, opened towards himself.

If Tom had been able to look over that winged shoulder, what might he have read in that book?

What the clock told him, Tom could not yet understand, and his mind turned away from it. He was back at thinking of the yew-tree he had seen over the yard-fence. 'That fence looked easy to climb,' Tom said to himself.

During the rest of the day, Tom matured his plan. He also wrote to Peter—the first of an important series of reports. He told Peter, as well as he was able, what had happened last night; he told him of his intentions tonight. He meant to climb into the next-door garden and examine the yew-tree there, because—surely—it was one of the trees that he had seen in his garden. He would go all round it; he would climb it; he would search it for any clue.

When he had finished his letter, Tom wrote across the top the initials: B.A.R. They stood for Burn After Reading. All Tom's letters to Peter, from now on, bore that direction. Only the picture-postcard of Ely tower was without it, and only that was not destroyed.

That evening Tom went to bed as usual, and kept deliberate watch. His uncle and aunt seemed so slow in going to bed and to sleep! Twice Tom dozed, woke with a start, and went to his bedroom door and looked out; and there was still a light from under the door of the other bedroom. The third time, it had gone; and, after the shortest wait that prudence required, Tom crept out and downstairs as before, to the hall. As he went along it, the grandfather clock began striking for what must be midnight.

'I hope the moon's well up, outside,' Tom thought. 'I shall need light for getting across the yard. It would be awkward to make a noise out there—falling over dustbins or the car or anything.'

The grandfather clock had reached the thirteenth stroke as he slid his fingers up the edge of the door to find the knob of the Yale lock. He could not find it. He felt again. There was no Yale lock.

He did not understand; but he tried the bolt. It had been shot home: that was how the door was fastened now. Now he knew—he knew! With trembling fingers he began to ease the bolt back into a well-oiled, rustless socket.

The grandfather clock was striking on and on. Upstairs Alan Kitson, wakened by it, humped his shoulders fretfully: 'It's midnight. What on earth does the clock think it's striking?'

His wife did not answer.

'Striking hours and hours that don't exist! I only hope it's keeping Mrs Bartholomew awake, too!'

But Alan Kitson would have been disappointed if he had seen Mrs Bartholomew. She was lying tranquilly in bed: her false teeth, in a glass of water by the bedside, grinned unpleasantly in the moonlight, but her indrawn mouth was curved in a smile of easy, sweet-dreaming sleep. She was dreaming of the scenes of her childhood.

And the grandfather clock still went on striking, as if it had lost all count of time; and, while it struck, Tom, with joy in his heart, drew the bolt, turned the door-handle, opened the door and walked out into his garden, that he knew was waiting for him.

V

The Footprints in the Dew

THERE is a time, between night and day, when landscapes sleep. Only the earliest riser sees that hour; or the all-night traveller, letting up the blind of his railway-carriage window, will look out on a rushing landscape of stillness, in which trees and bushes and plants stand immobile and breathless in sleep—wrapped in sleep, as the traveller himself wrapped his body in his great-coat or his rug the night before.

This grey, still hour before morning was the time in which Tom walked into his garden. He had come down

36

the stairs and along the hall to the garden door at midnight; but when he opened that door and stepped out into the garden, the time was much later. All night—moonlit or swathed in darkness—the garden had stayed awake; now, after that night-long vigil, it had dozed off.

The green of the garden was greyed over with dew; indeed, all its colours were gone until the touch of sunrise. The air was still, and the tree-shapes crouched down upon themselves. One bird spoke; and there was a movement when an awkward parcel of feathers dislodged itself from the tall fir-tree at the corner of the lawn, seemed for a second to fall and then at once was swept up and along, outspread, on a wind that never blew, to another, farther tree: an owl. It wore the ruffled, dazed appearance of one who has been up all night.

Tom began to walk round the garden, on tiptoe. At first he took the outermost paths, gravelled and box-edged, intending to map for himself their farthest extent. Then he broke away impatiently on a cross-path. It tunnelled through the gloom of yew-trees arching overhead from one side, and hazel nut stubs from the other: ahead was a grey-green triangle of light where the path must come out into the open again. Underfoot the earth was soft with the humus of last year's rotted leaves. As he slipped along, like a ghost, Tom noticed, through gaps in the yew-trees on his right, the flick of a lighter colour than the yew: dark—light—dark—light—dark . . . The lighter colour, he realized, was the back of the house that he was glimpsing, and he must be passing behind the line of yew-trees that faced it across the lawn.

His path came out by the asparagus beds of the kitchen-garden—so he found them later to be. Beyond their long, grave-like mounds was a dark oblong—a pond. At one end of the pond, and overlooking it, stood an octagonal summer-house with an arcaded base and stone steps up to its door. The summer-house, like the rest of the garden, was asleep on its feet.

Beyond the pond and the summer-house was another path, meandering in idle curves. On the other side of this path was a stretch of wilderness, and then a hedge.

Of the four sides of the garden, Tom had already observed that three were walled: one by the back of the house itself, another by a very high south wall, built of clunch blocks and brick; and another by a lower wall that might well prove climbable. A hedge, however, is almost always more easily passed than any wall; and Tom had no sooner got into his garden than he was curious to see outside it. Sharp-eyed, he searched the hedge for a way through: he only needed such a little hole for a push and a wriggle. Here was a narrow gap, at last; but, to his surprise, it led into the hedge instead of directly through it. From this entry a passage—about a foot wide and three feet high—had been worn along in the heart of the hedge. Tom crept along it.

The tunnel came to an end where there was another, bolder gap into the open, this time out on to the far side of the hedge. Tom found himself looking out over a meadow. There were cows in the meadow: some still at their night's rest; one getting up, hindlegs first; and one already at the day's work of eating. This last cow stopped grazing to stare at Tom, as though she thought she must still be dreaming. Stalks of grass hung from the sides of her mouth, and a long trickle of saliva descended from her lip and swung slightly in the little morning breeze that was getting up.

At the far side of the meadow a long, grey goose-neck rose from among the grasses, and Tom could see the bird's head turn sideways so that an eye could fix itself upon the gap in the hedge and the movement there. As a matter of fact, the look-out was a gander, although Tom did not know it; a moment later, the white necks of his wives rose round him, watching too. Then the gander strained his neck and breast upwards, and stretched his wings out into a splendid double curve—every pinion apart—and clapped them to and fro. First one goose and then another did the same, saluting the new morning.

Tom, made uneasily aware of the passage of time, crept back by the way he had come—back into the garden. He began to make himself familiar with it—its paths and alleys and archways, its bushes and trees. He noted some of its landmarks. At a corner of the lawn, a fir-tree towered up above all the other trees of the garden; it was wound about with ivy, through which its boughs stuck out like a child's arms through the wrappings of a shawl. On the high south wall, half covered by the sporting of a vine, there was a sundial; it was surmounted by a stone sun with stone rays, and its chin was buried in curly stone clouds —looking like his father's chin covered with shaving lather, Tom thought. To one side of the sundial, under a honeysuckle archway, was a door: Tom might have tried it, but the sight of the sundial, even without the sun upon it yet, had reminded him again of the passing of time. He hurried.

At the greenhouse, he did no more than look through the glass at the plants inside, and at the water tank, where a gleam came and went—perhaps a goldfish waking. The raised cucumber-frames by the greenhouse were walked round in less than a minute. He passed hastily along beside the aviary, where fan-tail pigeons were beginning to pick their way across the brick floor.

He criss-crossed the kitchen-garden beyond the asparagus beds: fruit trees and strawberry beds and bean poles and a chicken-wire enclosure where raspberry canes and gooseberry bushes and currant bushes lived sheltered from the attack of birds. Beside the gooseberry wire grew a row of rhubarb. Each clump was covered with the end of an old tub or pot drain-pipe with sacking over the top. Between the loose staves of one of the tub-ends was something white—a piece of paper. It was folded, and addressed in a childish hand—if one could call it an address: 'To Oberon, King of Fairies.' Tom certainly did not want to be mixed up with talk of fairies and that kind of thing; and he moved very quickly away from the rhubarb bed.

He came out upon the lawn again. Here were the flower-beds—the crescent-shaped corner-beds with the hyacinths, among which an early bee was already working. The hyacinths reminded Tom of his Aunt Gwen, but no longer with resentment. She knew nothing—poor thing! —and could be blamed for nothing, after all.

At the verge of the lawn, Tom stopped abruptly. On

the grey-green of the dewed grass were two clearly de-
fined patches of darker green: footprints. Feet had walked
on to the lawn and stood there; then they had turned back
and walked off again. How long ago? Surely since Tom
had entered the garden. 'I'm sure they weren't here when
I came out. Certain.'

How long had whoever it was stood there, and why?
He or she had faced the line of yew-trees opposite; and
that thought made Tom uneasy. When he had passed
behind those trees and seen the flick-flick-flick of the house
between them, had someone stood on the lawn watching
the flick-flick-flick of Tom as he went?

Tom looked at the house, letting his eye go from window to window. Had someone drawn out of sight at an
upper window? No, no: now he was just imagining
things.

Tom's nerves were on edge, and he actually jumped
when he heard a noise from up the garden. It was the
sound of a door opening. He took cover at once, and then
worked his way towards the sound. Someone had come
through the door in the sundial path—a man with a
wheelbarrow.

Tom took a moment to realize that this must be a gardener, and that he was doing nothing more sinister than
beginning a day's work. He was whistling; and now Tom
became aware that for some time the garden had been
filling with sounds—the sound of birds, the sound of leaves
moving in morning winds, and all the minute living,
breathing sounds of trees and bushes and plants and insects.
The sun's rays gleamed over all the garden, warming it to

life and sucking up the drenching dew; the sundial's iron finger threw a shadow at last, and told the time. Day was beginning, and Tom was afraid of being caught in a day-time not his own. Once again he crossed the lawn, this time with intent to get back into the house and upstairs to bed—if, indeed, his own room and bed were still there. He could see that the hall of the house was furnished with all the objects he had seen last night: the morning sun-shine lit them clearly. They looked forbiddingly real.

Fear made him hurry now; yet, even so, he paused on the threshold of the house and turned back to look at the footprints on the grass: they were still plainly visible, al-though the warmth of the rising sun was beginning to blur their edges. (It did not strike him as odd that his own foot-steps, which had crossed the lawn again and again, had left no similar trace.)

He went inside and shut the garden door behind him and bolted it. He had shut himself into absolute darkness; but he could still hear the ticking of the grandfather clock, and that gave him his bearings. He felt for a bracket to guide himself forward; unaccountably, he missed finding any bracket. He made for where the barometer should be; he found only a blank wall. Then he realized there was an emptiness all around him: the furniture had gone. Only the clock was left, but the clock was always there, time in, time out. It had been in the hall with the furniture and rugs and pictures; and now it was here in the bare hall of the daytime.

If the hall were as usual, then everything was as usual, and Tom was safely back in his own time, and his bed would be waiting for him upstairs. Yet now a lesser fear came to him, with a pang of conscience. The ticking of the grandfather clock reminded him. There was no thirteenth hour marked on the clock face; he had not that excuse for being out of bed. Nor had he been right in thinking this little expedition would take only a few minutes, anyway. He dared not think how much time he had spent in the garden: he had gone there before dawn; he had come away when the sun was up.

He went back upstairs into the flat and straight into the kitchen to consult the clock there. It was an ugly little clock, but it always kept perfect time.

He found the kitchen matches, and struck one, shielding both the sound of the striking and the flame—he had thought it wiser not to click on the electric light, lest even that might waken his uncle and aunt. He held the lighted match to the clock-face: the fingers pointed to only a few minutes past midnight.

Still only a few minutes past midnight!   NB.

Tom stared so long that the match burnt down, and he had to drop it. He was bewildered; but one thing he knew now: that he had not broken his promise to his uncle.

Tom tiptoed back to bed. He was right to make little noise, for his uncle was still only upon the edge of sleep. Alan Kitson had just finished a one-sided conversation begun a few minutes earlier. 'If that grandfather clock strikes one in anything like the way it's just struck twelve —on and on and on—then I'll go upstairs and knock Mrs Bartholomew up and complain. She needn't think *I'm* frightened of her.'

VI

Through a Door

EVERY night now Tom slipped downstairs to the garden. At first he used to be afraid that it might not be there. Once, with his hand already upon the garden door to open it, he had turned back, sick with grief at the very thought of absence. He had not dared, then, to look; but, later the same night, he had forced himself to go again and open that door: there the garden was. It had not failed him.

44

He saw the garden at many times of its day, and at different seasons—its favourite season was summer, with perfect weather. In earliest summer hyacinths were still out in the crescent beds on the lawn, and wallflowers in the round ones. Then the hyacinths bowed and died; and the wallflowers were uprooted, and stocks and asters bloomed in their stead. There was a clipped box bush by the greenhouse, with a cavity like a great mouth cut into the side of it: this was stacked full of pots of geraniums in flower. Along the sundial path, heavy red poppies came out, and roses; and, in summer dusk, the evening primroses glimmered like little moons. In the latest summer the pears on the wall were muffled in muslin bags for safe ripening.

Tom was not a gardener, however; his first interest in a garden, as Peter's would have been, was tree-climbing. He always remembered his first tree in this garden—one of the yews round the lawn. He had never climbed a yew before, and was inclined to think ever afterwards that yews were best.

The first branches grew conveniently low, and the main trunk had bosses and crevices. With the toes of his left foot fitted into one of these last, Tom curved his hands round the branch over his head. Then he gave a push, a spring and a strong haul on the arms: his legs and feet were dangling free, and the branch was under his chest, and then under his middle. He drew himself still farther forward, at the same time twisting himself expertly: now he was sitting on the bough, a man's height above ground.

The rest of the ascent was easy but interesting: sometimes among the spreading, outermost branches; sometimes working close to the main trunk. Tom loved the dry feel of the bark on the main trunk. In places the bark had peeled away, and then a deep pink showed beneath, as though the tree were skin and flesh beneath its brown.

Up he went—up and up, and burst at last from the dim interior into an openness of blue and fiery gold. The sun was the gold, in a blue sky. All round him was a spreading, tufted surface of evergreen. He was on a level with all the yew-tree tops round the lawn; nearly on a level with the top of the tall south wall.

Tom was on a level, too, with the upper windows of the house, just across the lawn from him. His attention was caught by a movement inside one of the rooms: it came, he saw, from the same maid he had once seen in the hall. She was dusting a bedroom, and came now to the window to raise the sash and shake her duster outside. She looked casually across to the yew-trees as she did so, and Tom tried waving to her. It was like waving to the He in blindman's-buff.

The maid went back into the depths of the room, to her dusting. She left the window open behind her, and Tom could now see more. There was someone else in the room besides the maid—someone who stood against the far wall, facing the window. The maid evidently spoke to her companion occasionally as she worked, for Tom could hear the faint coming and going of voices. He could not see the other figure at all clearly, except that it was motionless, and there was the whiteness and shape of a face that was always

turned in his direction. That steadfastness of direction em-
barrassed Tom. Very gradually he began to draw his head
downwards, and then suddenly ducked it below tree-level
altogether.

Tom saw more people later, in the garden itself. He
stalked them warily, and yet—remembering his invisibility to the house-maid—with a certain confidence too.

He was pretty sure that the garden was used more often
than he knew. He often had the feeling of people having
just gone—and an uncomfortable feeling, out of which he
tried to reason himself, again and again, of someone who
had *not* gone: someone who, unobserved, observed him.
It was a relief really to see people, even when they ignored
his presence: the maid, the gardener, and a severe-looking
woman in a long dress of rustling purple silk, face to face
with whom Tom once came unexpectedly, on a corner.
She cut him dead.

Visibility . . . invisibility . . . If he were invisible to the
people of the garden, he was not completely so at least to
some of the other creatures. How truly they saw him he
could not say; but birds cocked their heads at him, and
flew away when he approached.

And had he any bodily weight in this garden, or had he
not? At first, Tom thought not. When he climbed the
yew-tree he had been startled to feel that no bough swung
beneath him, and not a twig broke. Later—and this was a
great disappointment to him—he found that he could not,
by the ordinary grasping and pushing of his hand, open
any of the doors in the garden, to go through them. He
could not push open the door of the greenhouse or of the

little heating-house behind it, or the door in the south wall by the sundial.

The doors shut against Tom were a check upon his curiosity, until he saw a simple way out: he would get through the doorways that interested him by following at the heels of the gardener. He regularly visited the greenhouse, the heating-house, and used the south wall door.

Tom concentrated upon getting through the south wall door. That entry promised to be the easiest, because the gardener went through so often, with his tools. There must be a tool-shed somewhere through there.

The gardener usually went through so quickly and shut the door so smartly behind him, that there was not time for anyone else to slip through as well. However, he would be slower with a wheelbarrow, Tom judged; and he waited patiently for that opportunity. Yet even then the man somehow only made a long arm to open the door ahead of the wheelbarrow, wheeled it very swiftly through, caught the door-edge with the toe of his boot as he passed and slammed the door in Tom's face.

Tom glared at the door that once more was his barrier. Once more, without hope, he raised his hand to the latch, and pressed it. As usual, he could not move it: his fingers seemed to have no substance. Then, in anger, he pressed with all imaginable might: he knitted his brows, and brought all his will to bear upon the latch, until he felt that something had to happen. It did: his fingers began to go through the latch, as though the latch, and not his fingers, now, were without substance. His fingers went through the ironwork of the latch altogether, and his hand fell back into place by his side.

Tom stared down at that ever-memorable right hand. He felt it tenderly with his left, to see if it were bruised or broken: it was quite unhurt—quite as before. Then he looked at the latch: it looked as real as any latch he had ever seen anywhere.

Then the idea came to Tom that the door might be no more solid than the latch, if he really tried it.

Deliberately he set his side against the door, shoulder, hip and heel, and pressed. At first, nothing gave, either of himself or the door. Yet he continued the pressure, with still greater force and greater determination; and gradually he became aware of a strange sensation, that at first he thought was a numbness all down his side—but no, it was not that.

'I'm going through,' Tom gasped, and was seized with alarm and delight.

On the other side of the wall, the gardener had emptied his barrow-load of weeds and was sitting on the handle of his barrow, in front of a potting-shed, eating his midday dinner. If he had been able to see Tom at all he would have seen a most curious sight: a very thin slice of boy, from shoulder to foot, coming through a perfectly solid wooden door. At first the body came through evenly from top to bottom; then, the upper part seemed to stop, and the bottom part came through in its entirety, legs first. Then one arm came through, then another. Finally, everything was through except the head.

The truth was that Tom was now a little lacking courage.

The passing through the door of so much of his body had not been without enormous effort and peculiar, if indescribable, sensations. 'I'm just resting a minute,' said Tom's head, on the garden side of the door; yet he knew that he was really delaying because he was nervous. His stomach, for instance, had felt most uncomfortable as it passed through the door; what would the experience be like for his head—his eyes, his ears?

On the other hand—and the new idea was even worse than the old—supposing that, like a locomotive-engine losing steam-pressure, he lost his present force of body and will-power in this delay? Then, he would be unable to move either forwards or backwards. He would be caught here by the neck, perhaps for ever. And just supposing someone came along, on the far side of the wall, who by some evil chance *could* see him—supposing a whole company came: they would see an entirely defenceless stern sticking out—an invitation to ridicule and attack.

With a convulsive effort, eyes closed, lips sealed, Tom dragged his head through the door, and stood, dizzy, dazed, but whole, on the far side of it.

When his vision cleared, he saw that he was standing directly in front of the potting-shed and the gardener. Tom had never been front to front with the gardener before: he was a large-framed young man, with a weather-reddened face, and eyes the colour of the sky itself—they now looked straight through Tom and far away. Into his mouth he was putting the last fragments of a thick bacon-and-bread sandwich. He finished the sandwich, closed his eyes and spoke aloud: 'For all good things I thank the

Lord; and may He keep me from all the works of the Devil that he hurt me not.'

He spoke with a country voice, clipping short his t's and widening his vowels, so that Tom had to listen attentively to understand him.

The gardener opened his eyes again, and, reaching behind him, brought out another sandwich. Tom wondered, in some surprise, whether he said grace after every sandwich. Perhaps he never knew how many he was going to eat.

The gardener-went on eating, and Tom turned away to look around him. He was in an orchard, that also served for the keeping of hens, the pegging out of washing and the kindling of a bonfire. Beyond the orchard were meadows and trees, from among which rose the roofs of what must be a village.

While he looked, Tom was also keeping a sharp eye upon the gardener. When the man had really finished his meal he grasped the handles of his wheelbarrow, to return to his work in the garden. In a moment, Tom was beside him. He had not at all enjoyed the experience of going through a shut door, and he did not now intend to have to repeat it. This time there was an easy way through: he got nimbly up into the empty barrow and was wheeled back into the garden in comfort.

It was a long time before Tom literally forced his way through a door again. Anyway, he had seen the orchard, and that was enough in that direction; other doors could wait. Meanwhile, he climbed the low wall at the bottom of the garden and explored the wood beyond. On the third side of the garden he wormed his way through the hedge again and crossed the meadow. The only surprise there was the boundary: a river, clear, gentle-flowing, shallow, and green with reeds and water-plants.

The garden and its surroundings, then, were not, in themselves, outside the natural order of things; nor was Tom alarmed by his own unnatural abilities. Yet to some things his mind came back again and again, troubled: the constant fine weather, the rapid coming and going of the seasons and the times of day, the feeling of being watched.

One night all his uneasiness came to a head. He had gone from his bed in the flat upstairs and crept down to the hall at about midnight, as usual; he had opened the garden door. He had found for the first time that it was night, too, in the garden. The moon was up, but clouds fled continuously across its face. Although there was this movement in the upper air, down below there was none: a great stillness lay within the garden, and a heavier heat than at any noon. Tom felt it: he unbuttoned his pyjama jacket and let it flap open as he walked.

One could smell the storm coming. Before Tom had reached the bottom of the garden, the moon had disappeared, obscured altogether by cloud. In its place came another light that seemed instantaneously to split the sky from top to bottom, and a few seconds later came the thunder.

Tom turned back to the house. As he reached the porch, the winds broke out into the lower air, with heavy rain and a deathly chilling of the temperature. Demons of the air seemed let loose in that garden; and, with the increasing frequency of the lightning, Tom could watch the foliage of the trees ferociously tossed and torn at by the wind, and, at the corner of the lawn, the tall, tapering fir-tree swinging to and fro, its ivy-wreathed arms struggling wildly in the tempest like the arms of a swaddling-child.

To Tom it seemed that the fir-tree swung more widely each time. 'It can't be blown over,' thought Tom. 'Strong trees are not often blown over.'

As if in answer to this, and while the winds still tore, there came the loudest thunder, with a flash of lightning that was not to one side nor even above, but seemed to come down into the garden itself, to the tree. The glare was blinding, and Tom's eyes closed against it, although only for a part of a second. When he opened them again, he saw the tree like one flame, and falling. In the long instant while it fell, there seemed to be a horrified silence of all the winds; and, in that quiet, Tom heard something —a human cry—an 'Oh!' of the terror he himself felt. It came from above him—from the window of one of the upper rooms.

Then the fir-tree fell, stretching its length—although Tom did not know this until much later—along the grave-beds of the asparagus in the kitchen-garden. It fell in darkness and the resumed rushing of wind and rain.

Tom was shaken by what he had seen and heard. He went back into the house and shut the garden door behind him. Inside, the grandfather clock ticked peacefully; the hall was still. He wondered if perhaps he had only imagined what he had seen outside. He opened the door again, and looked out. The summer storm was still raging. The flashes of lightning were distant now: they lit up the ugly gap in the trees round the lawn, where the fir-tree had stood.

The tree had fallen, that had been a sight terrible enough; but the cry from above troubled Tom more. On the next night came the greatest shock of all. He opened the garden door as usual, and surveyed the garden. At first, he did not understand what was odd in its appearance; then, he realized that its usual appearance was in its itself an oddity. In the trees round the lawn there was no gap: the ivy-grown fir-tree still towered above them.

VII

Report to Peter

'Not unless you put the clock back,' Uncle Alan said carelessly, in answer to Tom's last question.

Tom doodled with his pen in the corner of the letter he was writing to Peter: a clock-dial, which he then enclosed at the top of a tall, rectangular case—a grandfather clock, in fact. He took some minutes to complete it; then he addressed his uncle again.

'What clock?'

'What did you say, Tom?'

'You said a tree could not be lying fallen at one time, and

then be standing up again as it was before it fell, unless you put the clock back. What clock?'

'Oh, no particular clock.' Tom scribbled out his sketch of the grandfather clock. 'It's just a saying, Tom—"to put the clock back". It means, to have the Past again, and no one can have that. Time isn't like that.'

His uncle returned to his reading; and Tom began doodling in another part of the writing-paper. After some time he found that he had drawn the shape of an angel-like creature with wings from his shoulders and with straddling legs. He had drawn the creature before he was aware, and then was startled at his own handiwork. He could not at once think whence the design had come into his mind. Then he remembered that it belonged to the grandfather clock and he scribbled that out too.

Then, 'What *is* Time like, Uncle Alan?' asked Tom.

His uncle put his book down altogether; and his aunt nervously put down her mending, too.

'Tom,' she said, 'you shouldn't always be asking such very odd questions of your uncle. He's tired after his day's work.'

'No, no, Gwen. A child's questions should certainly be answered. All I would object to Tom's questions is their lack of connexion, and sometimes of seriousness, too. Look at his first question: he asked whether it would be possible to go through a door—he actually asked *how* it would be possible!'

'Well!' cried Tom's aunt, with a relief that came from her not having paid attention to the earlier conversation. 'Well, that seems a very sensible idea—so sensible that it's almost silly!'

Alan Kitson raised his eyebrows, and his wife went on hurriedly: 'You know what I mean—going through a door's such an everyday happening.'

'Not when the door is shut . . . Then Tom went on to ask about the invisibility—the *invisibility*—of a person like himself.'

'Sometimes, in fairy stories——' Aunt Gwen began.

Tom shook his head indignantly.

'And finally,' his uncle continued, 'we have this question about a tree's being able to lie fallen one day, and then, on the next day, against all the known laws of Nature——'

'It was a dream!' interrupted Aunt Gwen, 'just a queer dream, wasn't it, Tom?'

'No, it wasn't!' Tom cried passionately. 'It was real!'

'Indeed!' said Uncle Alan, with slow relish. 'So this tree has really existed—this extraordinary incident has really happened! Tell us where, Tom, and when. Where and when, Tom?'

Tom remained silent. He dug his pen in a row of inky holes down the side of his paper.

'Come, Tom!'

'It was a fairy tree!' said Aunt Gwen, returning with desperate playfulness to her first suggestion. 'Goblin wood-cutters laid it low, didn't they, Tom?'

Uncle Alan smiled and picked up his book again. 'I am inclined to think you are right, after all, Gwen.'

'It fell in a storm,' Tom said in a strangled voice. 'Lightning struck it.' He looked at his uncle as if he would willingly have seen him struck in the same manner.

His aunt intercepted the look, and saw her husband's

mouth opening to speak. She rushed into the conversation again, and, this time, won: 'And now Tom mustn't speak again until he's finished his letter to Peter, nor be interrupted!'

So Tom went back to the letter, cramping his writing between the doodlings and stab-marks.

'. . . All I have told you is true,' he wrote, 'about the door and being invisible and the fir-tree. It is all very strange, but I don't *mind* any of it, except perhaps being invisible to everybody. For instance, there are three boys that have come into the garden. Their names are Hubert and James and Edgar. Edgar is about my age, but I think I would like James better. There is a girl who tags round after them. She is very young and is called Hatty or something . . .'

Without appearing to detach his attention from his book, Uncle Alan spoke: 'It's useless to write at length to anyone recovering from measles. After measles, the patient has to be particularly careful not to strain his eyes by overuse.'

'If Tom's letter is too long for Peter, then no doubt his mother will read it aloud to him,' said Aunt Gwen.

In alarm, Tom wrote 'PRIVATE' in the biggest capitals across the top of the letter, folded it intricately, and wrote 'Peter—PRIVATE' on both sides. He had to undo it again, to sign it, having forgotten that, in the panic. He then put the letter into an envelope, addressed it and wrote 'CONFIDENTIAL' in the top left-hand corner.

He found his uncle's eyes watching him ironically over the top of his book. Tom felt defiant. He licked the flap of the envelope and pressed it down. Then he drew the

outline of his long tom-cat across the edge of the stuck-
down flap. Like a seal, it guarded against any tampering.
Beneath the cat, Tom wrote: B.A.R.

Uncle Alan brought out his wallet. 'Here's a stamp for
your precious letter.' Tom thanked him stiffly.

The letter finished, Tom had nothing more to do. He
composed himself to wait patiently for bedtime. There
was no real use in his going to bed early: he could not go
down to the garden, anyway, until his aunt and uncle were
in bed and asleep.

His thoughts ran on the garden, as they always did nowadays. He reflected how dangerously near he had been to
betraying it, just now. Fortunately his uncle and aunt had
only laughed at him; if they had been more attentive and
sympathetic, he might have been trapped into telling more.
They might have found out his secret. The very next time
he visited the garden, they would have insisted upon going
with him . . .

Tom went chill at the idea.

'Are you feeling quite well, Tom?' asked his aunt.

'Yes, thank you, Aunt Gwen.'

Nevertheless, she fetched the thermometer and made
him put it into his mouth. 'You were shivering just now,
as if you had a chill.'

Tom shook his head.

'I hope it's not the onset of measles, for your sake, Tom.
It would mean your staying away from home several
weeks longer, perhaps, instead of only ten days.' She withdrew the thermometer and took it over to the light.

'Only ten days?' repeated Tom.

E

'I know you must be longing to get home,' said Aunt Gwen sadly; she would have liked him to have stayed much longer. Uncle Alan was saying nothing.

Only ten days! Only ten days more for the garden! 'I think perhaps I have a temperature, and it is measles,' said Tom. Surely, even with measles, he could still go down every night to the garden during those extra weeks while the disease ran its course.

'I can never find the thread of mercury at first,' Aunt Gwen was saying. She twisted and twisted the thermometer; then, at last, she held it still. 'No, Tom, you've no temperature, so you've no measles. That's a relief for you, isn't it? Home soon.'

'But——'

'Yes, Tom?'

He dared not say it: that suddenly he found that he did not want to go home. He wanted above all to stay here —here where he could visit the garden. His home now seemed a long, long misty way away; even Peter was a remote boy with whom he could only correspond by letter, never play. The boys nearer to him now were called Hubert and James and Edgar—James especially. There was a girl too—but she was only a girl. What had her name been? Hatty . . .

VIII

The Cousins

HUBERT was the eldest of the three boys Tom had seen in the garden. Indeed, in writing to Peter, Tom should perhaps hardly have called him a boy at all: he was, rather, a young man. Along his upper lip he already had dark, sparsely growing hairs, which he sometimes touched anxiously, appreciatively. He was already grown to man's height, although he had by no means properly filled out yet.

James, too, and even Edgar, were older than Tom. James's voice was a soft, hesitant growl, which, in the midst of speech, would occasionally slip upwards into a creaky treble, to his consternation. 'Oh!' he would say, and stop, and flush, in the presence even of his brothers.

The third brother, Edgar, had brindled hair and brindled brown eyes that moved round remarkably quickly, missing nothing. He talked quickly and sharply, too. Tom liked Edgar the least, although he was the nearest to him in age.

The three of them had walked from the house into the garden one day when Tom was already there. They were followed by a little girl in a frilled blue pinafore and with hair worn long to her shoulders. The only word you could have used about that child was 'tagging'. She tagged along after them, and then circled them every so often—in what might well have become an exasperating way—in order to face them and to listen to what they were saying. They were talking about a rat-shoot they were going to that evening: the miller had asked them to it; it was to be after dark, of course; and Bertie Codling would be there, and young Barty would come over too, perhaps; and they would take a hurricane lamp; and they would take their air-gun; and wasn't it a pity they hadn't an air-gun each, instead of only one between them.

Tom, from among the nearby trees, listened eagerly; and the little girl circled, and circled again.

'Let's all run from Hatty!' said Hubert suddenly, and at

once did so, his long legs covering great distances with each stride. James swerved away from her, too, laughing; and Edgar followed him. Hatty, as if she were used to such treatment, had already started a quick trot of pursuit, when Edgar turned and, stooping, flung before her the hazel-switch that he had been carrying. It did not touch her—it was not exactly meant to; but it made her stumble. She fell forwards on her face in the grass, and began crying.

James heard the sound, and turned back and picked her up. He shook her as he did so, but gently, saying, 'You juggins—you silly little juggins, you!' Tom, in justice to the girl, really could not see anything very silly in tripping over something suddenly thrown at your feet.

'What will aunt say?' wept Hatty, pointing to green grass-stains on her pinafore.

James batted at them with his hands, but, of course, that brought no improvement. Suddenly he seemed to lose patience. 'Why did you fall, then? You should look where you're going! I can't help you—I'm off with the others!' And he fled away after them, among the trees.

Hatty followed, sobbing to herself, but almost absent-mindedly. She went among the trees and paths, searching. Her eyes glanced continually hither and thither, and she soon stopped crying and carried her head in the position of one intently listening. Tom could see that there was some-thing expert in the way she looked for the three boys: this game had often been played before.

Tom decided to follow Hatty in her search.

She came across the gardener by the pond. 'Abel, have

you seen Cousin James, or Cousin Hubert, please? I don't want to find Cousin Edgar, though.'

'They didn't come as far nor this, Miss Hatty. Are they playing Catch with you again?'

'It's the only game they'll ever play with me.'

'Why don't you ask them to let you do the running away, for once, and they do the catching?'

'It would be no good: I can't run as fast as they can.'

'They could give you a start.'

She brightened: 'If they did, they wouldn't find me easily once I'd hidden. I could hide better than they do.' She became boastful, jumping about on her toes in front of the gardener. 'I know better secret places—many better secret places, and I can keep quieter than they can. So quiet, that nobody ever knows I'm in the garden at all.'

'Can you, now?' said the gardener, admiringly—to please her, Tom thought.

'I see everybody, and nobody sees me,' said the little girl. She was very cheerful now.

Suddenly, from the trees behind her, came a 'Coo-eee!' She turned, and Tom did likewise: Edgar was showing himself, to renew her pursuit.

Although she had said she did not want to find him, Hatty made for him at once. Almost immediately the other two boys broke cover. Together they all doubled back across the lawn towards the house. They would easily reach it before their pursuer, and Tom feared that he, as well as the unfortunate Hatty, would lose them. James was the last of the three runners, and Tom had taken to James: he was the kind of boy you might risk picking as a companion in tree-climbing or in any other pursuit. James was going rat-hunting that very evening——

'Hey!' shouted Tom, and, coming out into the open, put on a brilliant spurt in his running. 'Hey, James!' It was the first time he had ever shouted in the garden. Several birds rose in a flurry, but the boy he had called so loudly by name paid no attention. Tom overtook him, swerved across his path, calling him again as he did so: to James, Tom was invisible and inaudible. James pounded up the doorsteps and into the house and disappeared. All three had gone.

Tom was bitterly disappointed. He had not minded being invisible to the others—to the maid, and the severe-looking woman, and the gardener, and the little girl, and even to Hubert (who looked stupidly grown-up) and to Edgar (whom Tom actually disliked). But he would have liked to have made himself known to James: they could have been companions in adventure.

Stubborn against defeat, Tom followed more slowly, up the steps and into the house. He had gone in thus before, of course, every time he had gone back upstairs to his bed in the Kitsons' flat at the end of each visit to the garden. This time, however, he did not close the garden door behind him: he knew from experience that would shut him at once into the house of the flat-dwellers. This time he wanted the other house—the house that went with the garden.

So he left the garden door open, and advanced down the hall, past the wooden bracket and the barometer, towards the marble bracket and all the cases of stuffed animals and birds. He held his breath: perhaps, this time he would succeed in penetrating the interior of the night-time house, and explore it.

Although Tom moved quickly along the hall, intending to turn upstairs to where he heard (or thought he heard) the boys laughing among themselves—although he moved quickly, the furniture of the hall was dissolving and vanishing away before him even more quickly. Even before he reached the middle of the hall, everything had gone from it but the grandfather clock; and when he reached the middle, and could look sideways towards the stairs, he saw them uncarpeted, exactly as they were when his uncle and aunt and the others used them during the day. These were not the stairs that could ever lead him anywhere now but to bed.

'Bother!' said Tom. He turned back the way he had come, towards the garden door: through it the garden lay unchanged. As he stepped out over the threshold, he glanced back over his shoulder into the house: sure enough, the hall was re-filling behind him. Brackets, barometer, glass cases, umbrella stand, gong and gong-stick—they were all stealing back; and, of course, the grandfather clock had been there all the time.

Tom was vexed; but he resolved not to let this disappointment spoil his enjoyment of the garden. He would resolutely put James and the others out of his mind. He had already as good as forgotten the girl, Hatty. She had not come across the lawn and into the house after her cousins; for some reason, she had given up the chase. He did not wonder where she was in the garden now, or what she was doing.

IX

Hatty

Tom only rarely saw the three boys in the garden. They would come strolling out with the air-gun, or for fruit. They came for apples on the second occasion of Tom's seeing them, which was only a few days after the first.

With a terrier at their heels, they sauntered out of the house and—apparently aimlessly—took the path by the greenhouse, and so came into the kitchen-garden. Then, suddenly, they bunched together and closed upon a young tree of early ripening apples.

'We were only told not to pick any,' said Hubert. 'Come on, lads! Shake the tree and make them fall!'

He and James set their hands to the tree-trunk and shook it to and fro. An apple dropped, and then several more. Edgar was gathering them up from the ground, when he paused, looked sharply across to the bushes, and cried: 'Spying!' There stood the child, Hatty. She came out into the open, then, as concealment had become pointless.

'Give me an apple, please,' she said.

'Or you'll tell, I suppose!' cried Edgar. 'Spy and tell-tale!'

'Oh, give her an apple—she means no harm!' said James. As Edgar seemed unwilling, he himself threw one to her, and she caught it in the bottom of her pinafore held out in front of her. 'Only don't leave the core on the lawn, Hatty, as you did last time, or you'll get yourself into trouble, and us too, perhaps.'

She promised, and, eating her apple, drew nearer to the group. Each boy had an apple now, and they were eating them hurriedly, scuffling the earth with their feet as they came away from the tree, to confuse the tracks they had made.

Now they halted again—and it happened to be quite near Tom, but with their backs to him—while they finished their apples. The terrier snuffed his way round their legs and so came to Tom's side of the group. He was closer to Tom than he had ever been before, and became—in some degree—aware of him. So much was clear from the dog's behaviour: he faced Tom; his hackles rose; he growled again and again. Hubert said, 'What is it, Pincher?' and turned; he looked at Tom, and never saw him.

Edgar had turned quickly, at the same time: he looked more searchingly, through and through Tom. Then James turned, and lastly even Hatty. They all four stared and stared through Tom, while the dog at their feet continued his growling.

It was very rude of them, Tom felt, and very stupid, too. Suddenly he lost patience with the lot of them. He felt the impulse to be rude back, and gave way to it—after all, no one could see him: he stuck out his tongue at them.

In retort, the girl Hatty darted out her tongue at Tom.

For a moment, Tom was so astounded that he almost believed he had imagined it; but he knew he had not. The girl had stuck out her tongue at him.

She could see him.

'What did you stick out your tongue for, Hatty?' asked Edgar, who must be able to see things even out of the corners of his eyes.

'My tongue was hot in my mouth,' said Hatty, with a resourcefulness that took Tom by surprise. 'It wanted to be cool—it wanted fresh air.'

'Don't give pert, lying answers!'

'Let her be, Edgar,' said James.

They lost interest in the dog's curious behaviour, and in Hatty's. They began to move back to the house. The dog skulked along nervously beside them, keeping them between himself and Tom, and still muttering to himself deep in his throat; the girl walked slightly ahead of them all.

Tom followed, seething with excitement, waiting his chance.

They went in single file by the narrow path between the greenhouse and the large box-bush. Hatty went first, then the three boys. Tom followed behind the four of them; but, when he emerged from the path and came on to the lawn, there were only the three boys ahead of him.

'Where's Hatty?' James was asking. He had been the last of the three.

'Slipped off somewhere among the trees,' said Edgar, carelessly. The three boys continued upon their way back into the house.

Tom was left on the lawn, gazing about him in determination and anger. She thought she had slipped through his fingers, but she hadn't. He would find her. He would have this out with her.

He began his search. He looked everywhere that he could think of: among the bushes; up the trees; behind the heating-house; beyond the nut stubs; under the summer-house arches; inside the gooseberry wire; beyond the bean-poles . . .

No . . . No . . . No . . . She was nowhere. At last, behind him, he heard her call, 'Coo-eee!'

She was standing there, only a few yards from him, staring at him. There was a silence. Then Tom—not knowing whether he was indeed speaking to ears that could hear him—said: 'I knew you were hiding from me and watching me, just now.'

She might have meant to pretend not to hear him, as, earlier, she must have pretended not to see him; but her vanity could not resist this opening. 'Just now!' she cried, scornfully. 'Why, I've hidden and watched you, often and often, before this! I saw you when you ran along by the nut stubs and then used my secret hedge tunnel into the meadow! I saw you when Susan was dusting and you waved from the top of the yew-tree! I saw you when you went right through the orchard door!' She hesitated, as though the memory upset her a little; but then went on. 'Oh, I've seen you often—and often—and often—when you never knew it!'

So that was the meaning of the footprints on the grass, on that first day; that was the meaning of the shadowy form and face at the back of the bedroom, across the lawn; that, in short, was the meaning of the queer feeling of being watched, which Tom had had in the garden so often, that, in the end, he had come to accept it without speculation.

A kind of respect for the girl crept into Tom's mind. 'You don't hide badly, for a girl,' he said. He saw at once that the remark angered her, so he hurried on to introduce himself: 'I'm Tom Long,' he said. She said nothing, but looked as if she had little opinion of that, as a name. 'Well,' said Tom, nettled, 'I know your name: Hatty— Hatty Something.' Into the saying he threw a careless disdain: it was only tit for tat.

The little girl, with only the slightest hesitation, drew herself up into a stiffness, and said: 'Princess Hatty, if you please: I am a Princess.'

X

Games and Tales

TOM was half-inclined to believe her, at first.
Her gaze was very bright and steady; and, with her red
cheeks and long black hair and stiff little dignity, there was
perhaps something regal about her—something of a pic-
ture-book queen. Immediately behind her was the dark-

green background of a yew-tree. In one hand she held up
a twig of yew she had broken off in nervousness, or to play
with; in the other hand she held her half-eaten apple: she
held the two things like a queen's sceptre and orb.

'You can kiss my hand,' she said.

'I don't want to,' said Tom. He added, 'Thank you,' as
an afterthought, in case she really were a princess; but he
had his suspicions. 'If you're a Princess, your father and
mother must be a King and Queen: where's their kingdom
—where are they?'

'I'm not allowed to say.'

'Why not?'

She hesitated, and then said: 'I am held here a prisoner.
I am a Princess in disguise. There is someone here who
calls herself my aunt, but she isn't so: she is wicked and
cruel to me. And those aren't my cousins, either, although
I have to call them so. Now you know my whole secret.
I will permit you to call me Princess.'

She stretched out her hand towards him again, but Tom
ignored it.

'And now,' she said, 'I will allow myself to play with
you.'

'I don't mind playing,' said Tom, doggedly, 'but I'm not
used to playing silly girls' games.'

'Come with me,' said the girl.

She showed him the garden. Tom had thought that he
knew it well already; but, now, with Hatty, he saw places
and things he had not guessed at before. She showed him
all her hiding-places: a leafy crevice between a wall and a
tree-trunk, where a small human body could just wedge

itself; a hollowed-out centre to a box-bush, and a run leading to it—like the run made in the hedge by the meadow; a wigwam shelter made by a re-arrangement of the bean-sticks that Abel had left leaning against the side of the heating-house; a series of hiding-holes behind the fronds of the great ferns that grew along the side of the greenhouse; a feathery green tunnel between the asparagus ridges. She showed Tom how to hide from a search simply by standing behind the trunk of the big fir-tree: you had to listen intently and move exactly—and noiselessly, of course—so that the trunk was always between yourself and the searcher.

Hatty showed Tom many things he could not have seen for himself. When she was lifting the sacking over the rhubarb-tubs, to show him the sticks of rhubarb, Tom remembered something: 'Did you once leave a written message here?'

'Did you once find one?' asked Hatty.

'Yes—a letter to fairies.' Tom did not hide the disgust he had felt. 'Fairies!'

'Whoever could have put it there?' Hatty wondered. 'To fairies! Just fancy!' She pulled a grimace, but awkwardly; and she changed the subject quickly. 'Come on, Tom! I'll show you more!'

She opened doors for him. She unlatched the door into the gooseberry wire, and they went in. Among the currant bushes at the end they found a blackbird that must have squeezed in by a less official entrance, attracted by the fruit. The bird beat its wings frantically against the wire at their approach, but they manœuvred round it and then drove it

before them down the gooseberry wire and out—in a glad
rush—through the door they had left open. 'It's lucky we
found it,' said Hatty. 'I'm afraid that Abel . . .' She shook
her head. 'I really think he'd rather see birds *starving* than
eating his fruit.'

For Tom, she opened the orchard door from the sundial
path, and then the door into the potting-shed. Among the
tools and seed-boxes and flower-pots and rolls of chicken-
wire, they found a sack full of feathers—hen feathers and
goose feathers. Hatty dug her fingers in and threw them
up into the air in a brown-and-white storm so thick that
even Tom thought he felt a tickling on his nose, and
sneezed. Then Hatty crept over the floor, laughing, and
picked up all the fallen feathers, and put them back, because
otherwise Abel would be angry. Tom sat on the side of the
wheelbarrow and swung his legs and pointed out any stray
feathers still drifting down. He could not have helped
Hatty: he knew that, with both hands and all his force, he
could not have lifted even a feather's weight. Meanwhile
Hatty, on her hands and knees, seemed to have forgotten
that she was a Princess.

After that, they went to the little brick-built heating-
house, at the end of the greenhouse, and Hatty set about
opening that door for Tom. She was far too small to be
able to reach the flat square of iron that latched the top of
the door; but, standing on tiptoe and straining upward
with her yew-twig, she was finally able to poke it aside.
She opened the door, and they went down steps inside into
darkness and the smell of rust and cold cinders—the weather was so warm that the stove for the greenhouse was

not working. There was a small shelf with two or three books on it, that Hatty said belonged to Abel. The shelf was just out of reach, but they could see that the topmost book of the pile was a Bible. 'Abel says the Bible must be above all the other books, like—like the Queen ruling over all England.'

They went into the greenhouse, among the cacti and the creepers that swayed down from their roof-suspended cage-pots, and plants with strange flowers that could never be expected to live, like other plants, out of doors. Tom gasped for breath in the greenhouse, and wondered how they endured the stifling air. There was a Castor-oil Plant —Tom felt a little sick when Hatty named it. There was a Sensitive Plant, too, and Hatty showed Tom how, when she touched a leaf-tip, the whole frond drooped and shrank from her by folding itself together. The plant's sensitivity was something quite out of the ordinary; it seemed to feel even Tom's touch. He was so delighted that he worked his fingers over the whole plant, and left it in one droop of nervous dejection.

Then they leant over the water-tank and tried to see the goldfish—and tried to catch them. Hatty bared her arm, to plunge it in; and Tom laid his arm along hers and behind it, with his open hand behind hers, finger to finger. So, as with one arm and one hand, they dipped into the water and hunted. Tom could have done nothing by himself; but when Hatty very nearly caught a fish, Tom's hand seemed one with hers in the catching.

Then Hatty led Tom back to the doorway of the greenhouse and showed him the coloured panes that bordered the glass panelling of the upper half. Through each colour of pane, you could see a different garden outside. Through the green pane, Tom saw a garden with green flowers under a green sky; even the geraniums were green-black. Through the red pane lay a garden as he might have seen it through the redness of shut eyelids. The purple glass filled the garden with thunderous shadow and with oncoming night. The yellow glass seemed to drench it in lemonade. At each of the four corners of this bordering was a colourless square of glass, engraved with a star.

'And if you look through this one . . .' said Hatty. They screwed up their eyes and looked through the engraved glass.

'You can't really see anything, through the star,' said Tom, disappointed.

'Sometimes I like that the best of all,' said Hatty. 'You look and see nothing, and you might think there wasn't a garden at all; but, all the time, of course, there is, waiting for you.'

They went out into the garden again, and Hatty began to tell Tom about the yew-trees round the lawn. The one he had climbed and waved from was called the Matterhorn. Another tree was called the Look-out, and another the Steps of St Paul's. One tree was called Tricksy, because of the difficulty of climbing it: its main trunk was quite bare for some way up from the ground and could only be swarmed. Hubert and James and Edgar had all swarmed it in their time; Hatty could not swarm. (Tom felt superior—Princess or no Princess.)

Sometimes Hatty's information seemed doubtful to

Tom. They paused by a bushy plant, to which Hatty drew attention. 'This is the Burning Bush,' she said. She plucked a leaf, rubbed it between her fingers, and then held them up to Tom's nose.

He sniffed the finger-tips; the smell was of the faintest to him. 'Should it be a smell of scorching?' he asked doubtfully.

'No, James says the smell is of lemon-verbena.'

'Why is it called Burning Bush, then?'

'They say that if you come out at midnight on Midsummer Eve, and set a flame to this, the whole plant will blaze up.'

'How do you know—have you ever tried?'

'No, of course not. Because there's only one plant in the garden, and we don't want that burnt to ashes.'

'Oh!' Tom supposed to himself that it might be true.

Hatty drew nearer to him. 'Shall I tell you something —something secret?'

'If you like.'

'This bush is grown from a slip of the real burning bush —the one that burnt when Moses was there.'

'But that was long, long ago, and in the Bible!'

'I shan't tell you secrets again!' said Hatty, offendedly.

But she could never resist telling him. Not only on that first day of meeting, but on all the days following, her secrets and stories poured from her with haste and eagerness as though she were afraid that Tom's company would not be hers for long. When they were tired with playing in the garden, Hatty would lead the way to the summerhouse. They went up the steps and Hatty opened the door for them. From the back of the summer-house she brought forward two twisted iron garden chairs, and put them in the doorway, for herself and Tom. There they used to sit, looking over the oblong pond, watching the fish rise, and Hatty talked.

Once Edgar found them. They were not aware that he had been standing staring and listening, until suddenly—from one side of their view down the garden—he called to Hatty: 'What are you up to there, Hatty?'

'I am not "up to" anything, Cousin Edgar.'

'For the last five minutes you've been talking and nodding and smiling and listening, all by yourself.'

'I am not by myself. I am talking to a friend of mine.'

'Where is he?'

'On this other chair, of course.'

Edgar burst out laughing, very unpleasantly. 'Really, Cousin Hatty, people will think you're queer in the head —once it used to be fairies, which was just silliness; and now its somebody who isn't there!' He went off, laughing.

Hatty was trembling, when she turned back to Tom. 'And now he'll go and tell the others, and they'll jeer at me, and Aunt Grace will say it shows how unfit I am to go anywhere with other children, outside, in the village.'

'Well, then,' said Tom, 'why did you tell Edgar about me?'

She opened her eyes very wide at him: 'But one must tell the truth, mustn't one?'

Often, from their seat, they could see Abel at work down the garden. He would sometimes stop and look in the direction of the summer-house, and Hatty would then wave to him, in a Princess-like manner.

'So sad about Abel,' said Hatty, mysteriously.

'Sad?'

'The whole family is a sad one. But you must promise not to tell, if I tell you.'

Tom said nothing, and Hatty went straight on.

'He had just one brother, and they were together in the fields one day—it was just before Abel became gardener here. His brother was very jealous of him, and one day, in the fields, they fought. Well, really, his brother just attacked Abel—with a weapon—murderously.'

'Go on.'

'He killed Abel—that is, of course, he very nearly killed him. There was a great deal of blood. It lay smoking on the ground of the field.'

There was a horrified silence; and then Tom said suddenly, 'What was Abel's brother's name?'

'Really, I don't remember,' said Hatty, looking away from Tom at a bird in the sky.

'Was his brother's name Cain?' asked Tom. Hatty pretended not to have heard him. This was particularly irritating to Tom, as it was what he had to suffer from all the other people in the garden. 'Because the story of Cain and Abel is in the Bible, and Cain really killed Abel. I don't believe this Abel who gardens here has anything to do with the Bible Abel—except that he was called after him. I don't believe this Abel ever had a brother who tried to murder him.'

'Suppose I told you that Susan had told me—and Susan

is Abel's sweetheart? Or suppose I told you that Abel himself told me, as a secret?'

'I'm not sure you don't tell fibs,' said Tom; and even then he knew that he was choosing a mild word, to be kind to Hatty. 'I dare you to go to Abel now, and ask him whether he has a brother who tried to murder him!'

'I shan't ever—ever—tell you any more secrets—ever!' Hatty cried passionately; but Tom knew how much to fear that. Meanwhile, she did not take up his challenge to have the matter out with Abel, and Tom took this as permission to disbelieve her story. It was only a step from that to disbelieving that Hatty herself was the Princess she claimed to be.

Yet it was true that she had made this garden a kind of kingdom.

XI

The River to the Sea

'I MEANT to ask Hatty questions about the garden,' Tom wrote to Peter, 'but somehow I forgot.' He always forgot. In the daytime, in the Kitsons' flat, he thought only of the garden, and sometimes he wondered about it: where it came from, what it all meant. Then he planned cunning questions to put to Hatty, that she would have to answer fully and without fancy; but each night, when he walked into the garden, he forgot to be a detective, and instead remembered only that he was a boy and this was the garden for a boy and that Hatty was his playmate.

There was always so much to do in the garden. They were to build a tree-house in one of the yew-trees, as soon as Hatty could spy out some floor boarding for them; in the meantime, there were bows and arrows.

Hatty had said wistfully that Hubert and James and Edgar used to play at forest outlaws, with bows and arrows made in the garden.

'Why didn't you?' asked Tom.

'They said I was too young; and, then, when I was old enough, they said they were too old.'

'Well, why didn't you play by yourself? You could make your own bow and arrows.'

'I couldn't. I didn't know how. At least, I think I know how to make arrows, because James once showed me—they're easy; but not a bow.'

Then Tom told Hatty to get a sharp knife. She went indoors and came back with a kitchen-knife hidden under her pinafore. Directed by Tom, she hacked free a suitable stave of yew; it was unseasoned wood, but they could not help that. Then Hatty trimmed it roughly, and notched it round at either end for the bow string. She was clumsy with the knife at first, and Tom had even to explain to her about cutting always away from herself for safety.

When the yew stave was ready at last, Hatty found that she had not the strength to bend it and string it. Tom could not help her; and in the end she went to Abel.

Before stringing her bow for her, Abel examined its knifework.

'You did this, Miss Hatty?'

'Yes, indeed I did.'

'Aye, but who taught you to do it?'

'Someone.'

'Well, whoever it was taught you—take care he don't teach you trouble with it.'

'Trouble?'

'Trouble for yourself, Miss Hatty.' Abel gave her a long stare, which Tom, watching from a distance, could not understand. Then Abel strung the bow, as Hatty had asked.

Arrows were easy to make, and Hatty—as she had said—knew how. She sought out the straight, unknotted wands from among the old wood of the nut stubs. One end of each hazel-wand she trimmed and then notched, to fit on to the bow-string. The other end she capped and weighted with a short piece of elder. The cousins had always used elder, it seemed: you pushed the tip of the arrow into the elder pith until it held fast.

Tom wanted to have the arrows feathered; but Hatty was impatient to use them as they were, and Tom gave way. His only grief was that he could never shoot the arrows for himself. However, he gave advice.

He wanted Hatty to shoot at birds, but she refused, although—as he pointed out with truth—there was not the slightest danger of her ever hitting them. Instead, Hatty shot up into the air: she liked to shoot, and then screw up her eyes and watch the thin line of the arrow against the dazzling blue of the perpetual summer sky.

They lost four arrows in the tree-tops, from Hatty's

shooting upwards at random; and then the fifth arrow fell through the greenhouse roof.

The only witness of the accident, fortunately, was Abel; and he seemed to be on their side. In silence, he fetched a broom, to sweep up the broken glass, and a ladder and a spare pane of glass and some putty. When he had done the repair and had come down the ladder again, fear lifted from Hatty like a cloud—Tom could see that.

'Thank you,' she said to Abel. 'Aunt won't even know.'

'No,' said Abel. Then he said, with deliberation, 'But do you remember what I told you of.' It was not a question; it was not an order; rather, it was a warning, heavily foreboding.

'You mean,' said Hatty, after a moment's thought, 'about being taught trouble?'

Abel simply nodded, and walked away.

The next trouble they got themselves—or rather Hatty —into, was something from whose consequences Abel was powerless to save. The trouble had its first cause far back in their anxiety not to do more damage in the garden by arrow shooting. To avoid that, Hatty started a practice of shooting over the garden-hedge into the meadow beyond; then she and Tom would worm their way through the hedge tunnel, to retrieve their arrow.

They did no harm by going over the meadow, for it was already grazed close by cows. The search rather held up the archery; but Tom enjoyed the expeditions. So did Hatty; and, once the arrow was found, the river that bounded the meadow drew her like a charm. She even braved the geese in order to reach the river-bank.

The geese had goslings with them, now, and always fought a spirited rearguard action in their defence. Tom and Hatty did not want to drive them; but they did want to reach the river. They advanced slowly—Hatty slightly in the rear; the goslings steered far ahead, squeaking and making for the river, and the two geese went with them, and then, last of all, came the gander. He lurched along, his voice calling angrily, the feathers of his long neck rutted with anger, his head turning now to one side, now to the other, so that one eye was always backward-looking on his enemies. Every so often, he would slew round altogether and raise himself high to front them, and then suddenly drop his head and neck forward and down, almost level with the ground, and begin a snake-like run at Tom, hissing. It was always Tom he ran at, because by then Hatty would be well behind Tom and concealed by him as far as was possible.

The gander's run stopped short of Tom. He sheered off at the last instant, and went back to his waddling; he caught up with the geese and goslings and followed them, on the look-out, as before.

By this progress, the whole gaggle in time reached the river and launched themselves upon it. Then they swam up and down in the water—the elders squawking protests, the goslings rather forgetting the danger they were supposed to have been in. Tom and Hatty sat down on the river-bank, or wandered by it.

Hatty loved the river, but Tom was not very much impressed by it: he had seen other, bigger rivers; Hatty had not.

'This isn't big, for a river,' he said. 'And it looks shallow, and it has weeds in it.'

But Hatty, facing downstream, would say: 'You should see it farther down.'

'Have you?' asked Tom.

'No, but I've heard tell. The boys bathe in it only a little farther downstream, where there are pools; and they fish. It gets bigger as it flows downstream. It flows down to Castleford, and then it flows to Ely, and then it flows down and down into the sea, at last. So they say.'

'All rivers flow into the sea,' said Tom; but it was this particular river—the only one that she knew—that interested Hatty. She gazed eagerly downstream, as though she envied the waters their endless journeying.

'And sometimes, Tom, the river is big even here. Sometimes, in winter and spring, there are floods, and then the water brims right up the banks, and overflows them and comes flooding over this very meadow.'

'Hatty,' said Tom, curiously, 'if you like this river, why don't you go bathing in it, where the others do? Or why don't you paddle and wade here? Or you could get a boat and go downstream for yourself, and see where the river goes to.'

Hatty looked at Tom, startled, and said that she wasn't allowed in the meadow at all, just because of the river running by it. Her aunt said she might get her clothes muddied, or wet; or—most troublesome of all for everybody—she might even manage to get herself drowned.

Reminded in this way of her aunt, Hatty would jump up in a frightened flurry, and say she must get back into the garden; and nothing that Tom could say would dissuade her. She made her way quickly back over the meadow to the gap in the hedge. Tom followed. As the two of them left the river-side, all the geese and goslings came to land again, and clambered on to the bank. The three elders, and especially the gander, watched Tom and Hatty sharply. On each occasion they were there to see them take the secret way through the hedge.

The geese could not exactly be blamed for what followed. No, if anything, the arrow-shooting was to blame. The geese simply used their beady eyes to see the way that Tom and Hatty went with the retrieved arrow, and then, later, went that way themselves. Their motive was almost certainly curiosity and greed—kitchen-garden greed; not malice.

XII

The Geese

THE geese must have started their procession through the hedge into the garden soon after sun-up one day, for, when the dew was still thick on the grass of the lawn, there they were. Tom had stolen down from the flat at about midnight as usual; he had opened the hall-door, to find early morning outside in the garden; that had not surprised him, but the sight of the geese had.

The two geese and the gander raised their necks as usual

to stare at him, but the goslings paid no attention: they rambled over the lawn with uncertain interest; they plucked at the grass a little; one lowered his head to sip the dew. Several curved, white breast-feathers lay on the lawn, like little boats; and—far worse—there were one or two dark-green goose-messes.

'What will they say?' thought Tom, meaning Abel and Hubert and James and Edgar and Susan the housemaid and the severe woman whom he guessed to be Hatty's aunt— all the people he knew of. Hatty he did not include among the others, because he knew she must be indirectly responsible for this—she and her secret way through the hedge. Of course, Tom was to blame too: he admitted that freely to himself, and would have admitted it as freely to anyone who could have heard his voice.

There were soon others to see the geese besides Tom. First of all, Abel came along one of the paths to the lawn: he halted; his blue eyes opened very wide, aud his mouth too, but he stood speechless.

Then the sash of one of the bedroom windows went up, and Tom heard a commanding voice that he was sure belonged to Hatty's aunt. She called to Abel and asked what the geese were doing there—although at that moment it was only too plain to see—and what *he* was going to do and how they had got there anyway and especially—Tom's heart sank—who was to blame.

Abel began methodically to answer at least the first two questions, but, in the middle, the window was slammed down. There was a commotion of voices and footsteps upstairs, then coming down the stairs. It sounded like the whole household coming. Tom took cover behind a tree: in this kind of situation, the instinct to hide over-rode all his certainty of being unseen. He even felt uneasy that, in taking up his position, he had had to cross Abel's line ot vision for an instant.

Soon enough, they all came hurrying out of the house, on to the doorstep. Hatty was with them, attracted by the excitement, and not realizing its significance for herself. Hubert, James and Edgar hovered in the forefront, ready for action.

'Don't hurry them,' Abel was calling from the other side of the lawn. 'We'll drive 'em out into the orchard, where they can't do harm, and then I'll get 'em round into that old meadow again.'

Now Pincher the dog had arrived, last of all. He pushed his way through the legs of the group on the doorstep, and stood before them.

'Get the dog away,' called Abel. As he spoke he was slowly moving forward upon the geese, the three boys began the same movement, herding the geese in the direction of the door into the orchard. Nobody paid attention to Abel's warning about the dog; after all, he was remaining quietly upon the doorstep. Tom, however, could see that he had begun to shiver with excitement: he would not be able to restrain himself for long.

The geese were allowing themselves to be moved along, their heads high and ceaselessly turning, the goslings going ahead. The gaggle was suspicious, nervous, on the brink of panic. A sudden rush and barking of Pincher pushed them over that edge into a kind of goose-hell, that was

G

thereupon let loose. At once, instead of two geese and a gander, there seemed to be a dozen, making the noise of a hundred. White and grey wings at the stretch seemed to bar the whole lawn, and flailed the air. Geese, gander and goslings ran in the confusion of anger or terror, trampling over flower-beds, trampling over their own messes, trampling over each other—Tom saw the gander at one moment making a stand in defence of his young, with his enormous flat foot squarely on the back of one of them. Luckily, a large webbed foot is by no means as dangerous as a boot, and the gosling looked hardly flatter—though more flurried—afterwards.

Altogether, the only damage—but it remained considerable—was to the flower-beds and the lawn. Even the dog had had the sense to run clean through the storm of snapping beaks and round the outskirts and into the house again, its tail between its legs. Abel and the boys drew back a little, too: a frenziedly angry gander, with his wives by his side, and his goslings behind him and even under him, is a daunting sight.

So they waited until the gaggle had a little calmed itself; then—much more cautiously this time—they began to herd again. Hatty ran ahead to open the orchard door.

Tom stayed in hiding. There was nothing to be seen now except the devastated lawn, and, on the doorstep, one person remaining—Hatty's aunt. Tom had thought her stern-looking before; he liked the expression of her face even less now.

From their different positions, she and Tom heard what was going on. The goose-drivers reached the orchard door, and evidently the geese were safely got through, for there was a cry of triumph from one of the boys, and then the slamming shut of the door.

Then Tom expected to see them all coming back to the house; but they did not. He realized, in a moment, that they were making their way to the meadow-side of the garden, to find out how the geese had got in at all. As they went, there came occasionally the sound of a lamenting cry from Abel. Then their voices were heard along the meadow hedge. Then, at last, they reappeared on the lawn.

Hatty was not with them. Tom guessed that, now she knew her share of the blame, she had gone into hiding.

As the others came across the lawn, Abel raised his voice in the same deep, sad cry: he spoke of lettuces ripped to pieces by the geese, and of other plunderings; of seedlings trampled and broken; of goose-messes where they were least desired. And then, in answer to a sharp question from his mistress, he told of the gap and the tunnel in the hedge, through which the geese must have come.

'How they made that way unbeknownst is more than I know, unless the Devil himself taught them!' said Abel, with a grieving wonder.

'They didn't make it,' said Edgar suddenly. 'Hatty did.' It was only a guess, Tom was sure, but everyone saw at once the likelihood of the idea.

Abel stopped speaking abruptly, as though his mind had to go into reverse on the subject. The others were quiet too—so quiet that Tom, even from the distance of his tree, could hear the breathing of Hatty's aunt: it had become heavy and rasping.

'Harriet!' she called, so loudly and harshly that the sound was not like a woman's voice at all.

Hatty came out from hiding and walked across the lawn to her aunt, not quickly, not slowly. Her face was white, so that her eyes and hair appeared blacker than ever. Her face was quite white—Tom realized afterwards that even her lips had been colourless too.

She stopped in front of her aunt. Her aunt did not ask whether she had made the gap and the tunnel, and why; she asked none of the questions that Tom had expected; she asked no questions at all. She said: 'You are to blame.'

Hatty did not speak: it seemed to Tom that she could not. All the persons that her fancy had ever brought into this garden—Biblical heroes and fairies and the people of legend and hearsay and her own imagination—all her friends fell away from her now. Even Tom could not speak for her or lift a finger to help her.

He turned his face away, because he expected Hatty's aunt to strike her; but she did not. She spoke to Hatty instead: she called Hatty a charity-child, a thankless pauper that she had received into her home as a duty to her late husband, whose niece Hatty was; she said that only the claims of blood had induced her to take this mistaken pity upon Hatty; she had expected Hatty to be grateful and dutiful and obedient; and, instead, she was none of these things, but an expense and a shame to her aunt and her cousins—a liar, a criminal, a monster.

'Oh!' Tom whispered frenziedly to himself. 'Why

don't her mother and father take Hatty away—away?' He
believed no longer—he had not believed for a long time
—that Hatty's parents were a King and Queen; but surely
even the poorest, humblest parents would rescue their
child from this. His mother would; his father would—in a
great rush and roar of indignation that was made by their
love for him.

'Doesn't Hatty's mother know? Why doesn't Hatty's
father come?' He crouched and covered his face with his
hands, crying out at his own powerlessness.

He heard the cruel voice go on and on, and then, at last,
stop; and then nothing but silence. Unwillingly, after a
while, he raised himself and looked towards the house:
whether all of them, including Hatty herself, had gone
their ways in that silence, or whether they had all literally
vanished away—he could not say.

He walked away from the place where they had been,
down to the bottom of the garden, and climbed the low
wall there. He wandered among the trees beyond, and at
last sat down at the foot of one of them, and, in a kind of
exhaustion, fell asleep.

When he woke, he was aware of some difference in his
surroundings—a difference in time, he thought it to be.
Yet the sunshine through the leaves of the trees was still
coming from the east. It was still morning.

He went back over the wall into the garden and began
to look for Hatty or Abel or anybody but the dreadful
woman. Turning the corner into the sundial path, he saw
at the end of it a tiny little figure, all in black: a little girl,
half Hatty's size, in a black dress, black stockings, black

shoes. Even her hair was black, and had been tied with a black hair-ribbon. Now the ribbon had come undone and her loose hair fell forward over her face, and her hands were up to her face too, hiding it; she was sobbing into her hands.

Tom had never seen a grief like this. He was going to tiptoe away, but there was something in the child's loneliness and littleness that made him change his mind. This morning especially, for some reason, he could not say this was none of his business. He came up close to the child, and—it seemed silly, for no one but Hatty in all that garden had ever heard his voice—he spoke. 'Don't cry,' he said.

To his surprise, she did hear him: she turned slightly towards him, as if for comfort; but she did not cease her weeping, nor take her hands from her face.

'What are you crying for?' asked Tom gently.

'For home!' she wept. 'For my mother—for my father!'

Then Tom understood the meaning of the funeral black she was wearing and of that desolate, ceaseless crying. There was something else too—something almost unbelievable that he felt he would understand in another instant; something familiar in her voice and way of speaking; something in the way she *was* . . .

In the meantime: 'Don't cry,' he said helplessly.

'Oh, cousin!' she sobbed.

Then, with a little shake of the mind, Tom knew. She had mistaken him for a cousin—for Cousin Hubert or Cousin James or Cousin Edgar. This was Hatty, exactly the Hatty he knew already, and yet quite a different Hatty, because she was—yes, that was it—a *younger* Hatty: a very young, forlorn little Hatty whose father and mother had only just died and whose home was, therefore, gone—a poor, penniless, orphan Hatty who was being taken grudgingly into this house and family by an aunt whose love went no farther than her own three sons, and whose charity was as cold as her heart.

Now was not the time to startle this Hatty by showing her that he was not one of the cousins, after all; nor was it possible to comfort her. Tom said no more, but tiptoed away.

He never saw the little Hatty again. He saw the other, older Hatty, as usual, on his next visit to the garden. Neither then nor ever after did he tease her with questions about her parents. When, sometimes, Hatty remembered to stand upon her dignity and act again the old romance of her being a royal exile and prisoner, he did not contradict her.

XIII

The Late Mr Bartholomew

IN the Kitsons' flat Time was not allowed to dodge about
in the unreliable, confusing way it did in the garden
—forward to a tree's falling, and then back to before the
fall; and then still farther back again, to a little girl's first
arrival; and then forward again. No, in the flat, Time was
marching steadily onwards in the way it is supposed to go:
from minute to minute, from hour to hour, from day to
day.

The day for Tom's going home had already come and
gone; but he was still staying with his aunt and uncle. He
had managed that for himself: the very day before he was
due to go, he had nerved himself, cleared his throat and
said, 'I wish I hadn't to go home tomorrow.'

Uncle Alan had been reading the newspaper; the sheets
crumpled down on to his knees, as though his hands no

longer had the strength to hold them. His eyes refocused from the print on to Tom: 'What?'

'I wish I hadn't to go home tomorrow,' said Tom. He dared not go farther, but he spoke loudly. Aunt Gwen gave a cry of amazement and delight, and actually clapped her hands. 'Would you like to stay?'

'Yes.'

'Several days more? Another week?'

'Or more,' said Tom.

'We'll send a telegram at once,' said Aunt Gwen, and ran out.

Tom and his uncle were left together. Alan Kitson studied Tom with intent curiosity. 'Why do you want to stay here?'

'I won't, if you'd rather not,' said Tom, with pride; but his heart sank at the thought.

'No ... No ...' Uncle Alan still watched him. 'But I wondered why. ... What is there to interest a boy here —to pass his time even?'

'I just like it here,' Tom muttered.

Aunt Gwen came back from sending her telegram to Tom's parents. Her face was flushed; she spoke fast and eagerly: 'We'll go about and see the sights and go excursions—we'll do so much now you're out of quarantine and staying on. You needn't be cooped up dully indoors any longer, Tom.'

Tom said, 'Thank you'; but without enthusiasm. He would have much preferred to be left to dullness indoors, as he used to be. He lived his real and interesting life at night-time, when he went into the garden; in the daytime, he wanted only peace—to think back and to think forwards, always to the garden; to write of the garden to Peter. He did not want to sleep, but, all the same, the daytime in the flat was like a period of sleep to him. He needed its rest.

Aunt Gwen arranged several expeditions to the shops and to the museum in Castleford and the cinema. Tom bore them patiently. He liked the cinema best, because he was in the dark, and so he could sit with his eyes shut and think his own thoughts.

Towards the end of Tom's lengthened stay, the weather changed for the worse. Still Aunt Gwen obstinately insisted on treats and trips, now with waterproofs and umbrella. After a visit to the cinema, she and Tom had been obliged to wait for some time for the bus, and Tom had stood in a puddle. It was his aunt who noticed his position, and that only as the bus came: 'Tom, you've been standing in a puddle all this time—quite a deep puddle!' He was surprised: his head had been in the clouds—in the white clouds that pile above an eternally summer garden —and he had not been noticing his feet at all. Now that he thought of them, they certainly felt very damp and cold.

'I hope you don't catch cold,' his aunt said anxiously. In answer to this, Tom sneezed.

His aunt rushed him home to a hot drink and a hot bath and bed; but a cold, once it has its fingers on its victim, will seldom loosen its grip before the due time. So Tom had a severe cold, that kept him in bed for several days, and indoors for many more. His convalescence was not hurried.

Gwen Kitson wrote happily to her sister that Tom would not be fit to travel for some time yet; and Tom wrote to Peter, 'It's a wonderful piece of luck—the next best thing to measles.'

Every night he was able to steal downstairs as usual, into the garden; and there the feverishness of his chill always left him, as though the very greenness of trees and plants and grass cooled his blood. He played with Hatty.

In the daytime he lay back among his pillows, deliberately languid. Uncle Alan, who was touched by the idea of a sick child, offered to teach him chess; but Tom said he did not feel clear-headed enough. He did not want to talk; and he allowed his aunt to see that he was certainly not up to being read to from schoolgirl adventures.

At the beginning of Tom's illness, his head had really felt a little light; and his eyelids gummed themselves up easily. He did not mind keeping them closed: then, in his imagination, he could look into his garden and see, in fancy, what Hatty might be doing there.

His aunt would tiptoe into his bedroom and look at him doubtfully. She would test whether he were awake by a whispering of his name. The voice recalled him, without his understanding at once to what: his eyelids opened on to his own bedroom, but his eyes printed off the shadowy figure of Hatty against the barred window and the cupboard and between himself and the figure of his aunt at the foot of the bed.

Hatty's image haunted the room for Tom, at this time; and so it was, perhaps, that he began, at first idly, then seriously, to consider whether she herself were not, in some unusual way, a ghost. There was no one who knew her ghost story and could tell it to Tom, so he began trying to make it up for himself: Hatty had lived here, long, long ago—in this very house, with the garden he knew of; here she had lived, here died . . .

From below sounded the striking of Mrs Bartholomew's grandfather clock, that knew secrets but would not tell them. Listening, Tom suddenly caught his breath: Mrs Bartholomew, of course! She, of all people, might know something of the past history of this house; or rather, there must once have been a Mr Bartholomew, and his family had perhaps owned this house for generations, and therefore he had known all about it. He would surely have told his wife the history of it, which she would still remember.

Tom resolved that, as soon as he was better, he would call on Mrs Bartholomew. True, she was an unsociable old woman of whom people were afraid; but Tom could not let that stand in his way. He would boldly ring her front door bell; she would open her front door just a crack and peer crossly out at him. Then she would see him, and at the sight of his face her heart would melt (Tom had read of such occurrences in the more old-fashioned children's books; he had never before thought them very probable, but now it suited him to believe): Mrs Bartholomew, who did not like children, would love Tom as soon as she saw his face. She would draw him inside at once, then and there; and later, over a tea-table laden with delicacies for him alone, she would tell Tom the stories of long ago. Sometimes Tom would ask questions, and she would answer them. 'A little girl called Harriet, or Hatty?' she would say, musingly. 'Why, yes, my late husband told me once of such a child—oh! long ago! An only child she was, and an orphan. When her parents died, her aunt took her into this house to live. Her aunt was a disagreeable woman . . .'

So the story, in Tom's imagination, rolled on. It became confused and halting where Tom himself did not already know the facts; but, after all, he would only have to wait to pay his call upon Mrs Bartholomew, to hear it all from her own lips. She would perhaps end her story, he thought, with a dropping of her voice: 'And since then, Tom, they say that she and her garden and all the rest haunt this house. They say that those who are lucky may go down, about when the clock strikes for midnight, and open what was once the garden door and see the ghost of that garden and of the little girl.'

Tom's mind ran on the subject. His cold was getting so much better now that his aunt and uncle had insisted on coming to sit with him, to keep him company. One day, hardly speaking aloud, Tom began a sentence: 'When Mr Bartholomew lived in this house——'

'But I don't think Mr Bartholomew ever did live here,' said Aunt Gwen. 'Do you, Alan?'

Uncle Alan did not answer at first, being in the depths of a chess problem in which he had failed to interest Tom.

'But, Aunt Gwen,' Tom protested, 'this was his family home. How else would he have known the history of this house, and the ghost stories too? How else could he have told Mrs Bartholomew?'

'Why, Tom——' said his aunt, in bewilderment.

'Mr Bartholomew, whoever he was, never lived in this house,' Uncle Alan now said positively. 'Mrs Bartholomew was a widow when she came here; and that wasn't so many years ago, either.'

'But what about the clock?'

'What clock?'

'The grandfather clock in the hall. You said it belonged to Mrs Bartholomew; but that clock has always been in this house. It was here long, long ago—it was here when the house had a garden.'

'Now, what reason have you for supposing all this, Tom?' asked Uncle Alan. He spoke less sharply than usual, because he really thought the boy must be feverish.

Tom was searching in his mind for an explanation that yet would not give away his secret, when his aunt came unexpectedly to his rescue. 'You know, Alan, the clock certainly must have been here a long time, because of its screws at the back having rusted into the wall.'

'Well, now, Tom, that might explain a little,' said Uncle Alan. He patted Tom's hand, as it lay on the counterpane, to soothe him. 'The clock may well have been here a long time, as you say, and during that time the screws rusted up. After that happened, the clock couldn't be moved without danger of damaging it. When old Mrs Bartholomew came, she had to buy the clock with the house. You see, Tom? It's all quite straightforward, if you reason it out.'

From that time, abruptly, Tom ceased to hope for anything from Mrs Bartholomew.

The possibility of Hatty's being a ghost stayed in his

mind, however—at the back of his mind. He was not even aware of the presence of the idea, until one day in the garden it became the cause of a quarrel with Hatty herself. It was the only real quarrel that ever took place between them.

They were beginning to build their tree-house, in the Steps of St Paul's; as usual, Tom was directing, while Hatty did the work of pulling and plaiting branches together, to make the walls. The floor—of old pieces of boarding that Hatty had found in the potting-shed—was already in place.

Hatty, as she worked, was singing to herself from hymns and songs and ballads. Now she was singing the end of the ballad of Sweet Molly Malone:

> 'Her ghost wheels her barrow
> Through streets broad and narrow,
> Singing, "Cockles and Mussels,
> Alive—alive-oh!" '

And Hatty continued to hum and murmur, under her breath, the refrain: 'Alive—alive-oh! Alive—alive-oh!'

Suddenly Tom said—he blurted it out before he could help himself: 'What's it like—I mean, I wonder what it's like to be dead and a ghost?'

Hatty stopped singing at once, and looked at him slyly over her shoulder, and laughed. Tom repeated the question: 'What is it like to be a ghost?'

'Like?' said Hatty. She turned fully to face him, and laid a hand upon his knee, and looked eagerly into his face. 'Ah, tell me, Tom!'

For a moment, Tom did not understand her; then he jumped to his feet and shouted: 'I'm not a ghost!'

'Don't be silly, Tom,' Hatty said. 'You forget that I saw you go right through the orchard door when it was shut.'

'That proves what I say!' said Tom. 'I'm not a ghost, but the orchard door is, and that was why I could go through it. The door's a ghost, and the garden's a ghost; and so are you, too!

'Indeed I'm not; you are!'

They were glaring at each other now; Hatty was trembling. 'You're a silly little boy!' she said (and Tom thought resentfully that she seemed to have been growing up a good deal too much recently). 'And you make a silly little ghost! Why do you think you wear those clothes of yours? None of my cousins ever played in the garden in clothes like that. Such outdoor clothes can't belong to nowadays, I know! Such clothes!'

'They're my pyjamas,' said Tom, indignantly, 'my best visiting pyjamas! I sleep in them. And this is my bedroom slipper.' His second slipper had been left, as usual, to wedge the flat-door upstairs.

'And you go about so, in the daytime, always in your night-clothes!' Hatty said scornfully. 'And it's the fashion nowadays, is it, to wear only one slipper? Really, you are silly to give such excuses! You wear strange clothes that no one wears nowadays, because you're a ghost. Why, I'm the only person in the garden who sees you! I can see a ghost.'

Hatty would never believe the real explanation of his clothes, and Tom chose what he thought was a shorter counter-argument: 'Do you know I could put my hand through you—now—just as if you weren't there?'

Hatty laughed.

'I could—I could!' shouted Tom.

She pointed at him: 'You're a ghost!'

In a passion, Tom hit her a blow upon the outstretched wrist. There was great force of will as well as of muscle behind the blow, and his hand went right through—not quite as through thin air, for Tom felt a something, and Hatty snatched back her wrist and nursed it in her other hand. She looked as if she might cry, but that could not have been for any pain, for the sensation had not been strong enough. In a wild defence of herself, Hatty still goaded him: 'Your hand didn't go through my wrist; my wrist went through your hand! You're a ghost, with a cruel, ghostly hand!'

'Do you hear me?' Tom shouted. 'You're a ghost, and I've proved it! You're dead and gone and a ghost!'

There was a quietness, then, in which could be heard a cuckoo's stuttering cry from the wood beyond the garden; and then the sound of Hatty's beginning softly to weep. 'I'm not dead—oh, please, Tom, I'm not dead!' Now that the shouting had stopped, Tom was not sure of the truth, after all, but only sure that Hatty was crying as he had never seen her cry since she had been a very little girl, wearing mourning-black and weeping her way along the sundial path—weeping for death so early.

He put his arm round her: 'All right, then, Hatty! You're not a ghost—I take it all back—all of it. Only don't cry!'

H

He calmed her; and she consented at last to dry her tears and go back to plaiting the branches, only sniffing occasionally. Tom did not reopen a subject that upset her so deeply, although he felt that he owed it to himself to say, some time later, 'Mind you, I'm not a ghost either!' This, by her silence, Hatty seemed to allow.

XIV

The Pursuit of Knowledge

A<small>ND</small> yet, in spite of his assurance to Hatty, Tom continued secretly to consider the possibility of her being
a ghost, for two reasons: firstly, that there seemed no other
possibility; and secondly—and Tom ought to have seen
that this was the worst kind of reason—that if Hatty weren't
a ghost, then perhaps that meant he was. Tom shied away
from that idea.

On the afternoon of the quarrel he had been impressed
—although he had been careful to hide this from Hatty—

by her method of argument. She had a girl's quick eye for clothes, and she had used it, on this occasion, against him. Tom wished that he were able to do the same kind of thing; but he found that he remembered only vaguely the appearance of the people of the garden. He had, it was true, a strong general impression that they were not dressed like himself and his aunt and uncle; but 'old-fashioned' was the nearest that he could get to the difference. Both Susan the maid and Hatty's aunt, for instance, had worn skirts nearly to the ground.

Naturally their clothes would be old-fashioned, if Hatty were a ghost. Yet to prove her that, he must be able to put an exact date to the clothes in the garden, and so to Hatty herself.

He thought he knew where he could find information. He had often noticed on his aunt's kitchen shelf, together with Mrs Beeton's and all the other cookery books, a volume invitingly called *Enquire Within Upon Everything*. Now, when his aunt was out shopping, he slipped out of bed and borrowed it.

He looked in the Index for CLOTHING—Styles of Clothing in the Past. There was nothing under STYLES, or under PAST. Under CLOTHES there were subheadings that Tom would certainly have found interesting at any other time —Loose Warmer than Tight, and Rendering Fireproof; but there was nothing about the changing fashions of history. He felt dispirited, as though he had been invited to call, and promised a feast, and then, when he had knocked at the door, found no one *Within*.

Before he shut the book, however, Tom came by chance

across something that proved useful in another way. On a page headed kindly 'The Good is Oft Interred with their Bones', he found a list of the Monarchs of England from the Norman Conquest to the Present. He remembered that Hatty had once mentioned a monarch of England. They had been looking at Abel's little pile of books in the heating-house; and Hatty had pointed out that the topmost book was a Bible, because Abel believed in the Bible being above all, 'like the Queen ruling over all England'. Hatty, then, lived when a Queen, not a King, ruled in England. Tom consulted his list of Monarchs: there had been very few Queens in the past. The possibilities suddenly narrowed: Hatty couldn't, for instance, have lived in the twelfth, thirteenth, fourteenth or fifteenth centuries at all, because there had only been Kings then, according to *Enquire Within*. For the same reason, she could not have lived in most of the seventeenth or eighteenth centuries. That left the other parts of those centuries, and most of the sixteenth and nineteenth centuries.

Tom returned *Enquire Within*, and, on the next occasion of his being left alone in the flat, prowled round looking for any other book of useful information. In his uncle's and aunt's bedroom he had a find: a complete set of volumes of the *Encyclopaedia Britannica* in their own special glass-fronted bookcase, kept to hand on Uncle Alan's side of the bed.

Tom looked up CLOTHING, and that asked him to 'See COSTUME', which he did. There were many pages in double columns of small print, whose appearance somehow discouraged him. He preferred to look at the pictures, although none of them really corresponded with what was worn by the people of his garden.

He noticed an oddity in the earlier illustrations. The men wore various kinds of leg coverings, but never trousers: the first pair of trousers to be represented was worn by a French Man of Fashion in the Early Victorian Period. Tom did at least know that the men and boys in his garden had all worn trousers—with the exception of Edgar, who sometimes wore a kind of breeches with woollen stockings.

Hot on the scent now, Tom turned to the volume TON to VES of the *Encyclopaedia*, and looked up TROUSERS. There were no illustrations, but the written account was short. In order to clear up any misunderstanding, it began by defining trousers: 'the article of dress worn by men, covering each leg separately and reaching from the waist to the foot'. Well, Tom agreed to that, and read carefully on. The wearing of trousers, it seemed, had been introduced in the early nineteenth century; the Duke of Wellington had caused a sensation with his. The article ended: 'Strong opposition was taken against them by the clergy and at the universities. (See COSTUME.)'

Tom now felt he had enough information to arrange into an argument. 'Hatty lived when men wore trousers, so she can't have lived earlier than the nineteenth century, when trousers came into fashion. Very well.' He remembered *Enquire Within*: 'And there was a Queen ruling in England in the nineteenth century: Queen Victoria 1837 to 1901. She must be Hatty's queen. And then there's the French Man of Fashion in trousers: he belonged to the

Early Victorian Period. That's where Hatty belongs. That Period is over a hundred years ago, so, if Hatty were a girl then, she must be dead by now, and all I can have seen in the garden is a ghost.'

The proof seemed final to Tom; but he double-checked it with a question in just the way that would, he thought, have delighted his uncle. What about the long skirts worn by the women of the garden? When had *they* been in fashion?

By now Aunt Gwen was back from her shopping and Tom was innocently back in bed. He tried her with his question; she answered promptly: 'Why, Tom, long skirts were always the fashion, until not so long ago. Up to the First World War, certainly.'

'Would women have been wearing long skirts at, say, the beginning of Queen Victoria's reign?'

'Oh, yes; all during Victoria's reign, and after,' said his aunt. 'Why, there must be many people alive today who remember long skirts well!'

Tom, however, was not at all interested in how recently such skirts had been the fashion; he was intent upon a remote Past, and in proving that Hatty had belonged to it, and was now a ghost—a little Early Victorian ghost. Well, all his information surely pointed that way. The question having been settled to his satisfaction, he put it out of his mind.

XV

The View from the Wall

IN following the course of Tom's historical researches and
his reasoning, we have gone a little ahead upon the

order of events—as Tom perceived them—in the garden. The tree-house in which he and Hatty quarrelled was not built immediately after the episodes of the geese upon the lawn and the little girl in mourning. Indeed, on his next visit to the garden after those happenings, Tom thought for a time that he had lost Hatty for good. The garden appeared absolutely deserted.

He called, and searched through all the usual hiding-places. He dashed round and round the trunk of the fir-tree, imagining he heard her slippers moving nimbly on the dry earth the other side, always evading him. But if Hatty had hidden, she had hidden better than ever before, and made the garden seem a green emptiness.

He saw over the south wall a thread of smoke that mounted vertically into the soft, still summer air, and it occurred to him that Abel was perhaps tending his bonfire. He stopped dead by the orchard door, wondering whether he should thrust himself through it again. If Abel were the other side he might provide some clue to Hatty's whereabouts.

Suddenly the orchard door opened and Hatty came through. At once all Tom's anxiety turned to annoyance, especially as Hatty looked far from anxious—excited, rather; even pleased. Her face was flushed, and there was a bonfire smut on one cheek; she held something in her pinafore pocket.

'Why didn't you answer?' Tom demanded. 'Didn't you hear me? I called and called and called.'

'I was helping Abel with his bonfire.'

'You could just have come and opened the orchard door and let me through. I like bonfires, too.'

'You wouldn't have liked this bonfire—you wouldn't have liked what we were burning on it.' She looked at him defiantly.

'Well, what were you burning on it?'

Now she lost courage, and cast her eyes down; but finally said: 'The bow and arrows. Oh, Tom, it was Abel who wanted to have them burnt!'

Tom was silent, guessing why Abel had wished it: he had always said that the bow might bring trouble to Hatty; and, indeed, it had done.

Hatty went on, 'And, as well as that, he wanted me to promise not to borrow any more knives from the kitchen, because they're so sharp and might cut and hurt me. And if I promised to let him burn the bow and arrows and if I promised not to use the kitchen-knives again, he said he'd give me a little knife all of my own.'

'What kind of knife?'

She brought her hand out of her pinafore pocket, and opened it: across the palm lay a gaudy, cheap little pen-knife, ornamented with true-love-knots in blue. 'He bought it at the Fair, to give to Susan; but she wouldn't have it from him, because it's unlucky to have a knife from your sweetheart. So Abel gave it to me. It's a dear little knife.' She turned it over lovingly.

'Open it,' ordered Tom. Hatty did so, and held it towards him so that he could see the blade—there was only one.

'Well!' Tom laughed shortly. 'You certainly couldn't

cut yourself with that! You could just about cut butter with it, that's all!'

Hatty was still admiring the coloured decoration of the haft; but she said, 'I've cut more than butter with it, already. Come, and I'll show you.'

There was a touch of mystery and pride with which she took Tom to one of the yew-trees—it was the one called Matterhorn—and showed him the tree-trunk on which were carved—or, rather, half scratched, half pressed—the initials: 'H. M.'

Tom was wondering what surname the 'M' stood for, but not liking to ask, when Hatty said: 'That means: "*Hatty Melbourne* has climbed this tree." With my knife, I've carved my initials on all the yew-trees—except for Tricksy, of course.'

'It's very wrong to carve things on trees,' said Tom, remembering suddenly to be severe. 'It's like leaving litter about.'

Hatty opened her eyes wide, as though, she had never heard of litter; and Tom could tell by her expression that she didn't think her carving could be wrong, on *her* trees, and anyway, she intended to go on doing it if she liked, without telling him.

'And,' Tom pointed out, 'you'll only get yourself into trouble if anyone sees those tree-trunks. They'll see "H. M.", and they'll know they're your initials, and they'll know you're to blame. Now, if I wanted to carve my mark on a tree—which, of course, I wouldn't, ever—but if I wanted to, I'd make a secret mark.' He told her of his device of the long tom-cat, for Tom Long.

Hatty was envious. 'Melbourne's such a stupid name.'

'There's Hatty,' said Tom. 'You could draw a hat.'
Hatty's eyes sparkled. 'Only, of course, you mustn't—
I've told you why not. And now,' he said, suddenly tiring
of talk, 'let's do something.'

'Let's,' agreed Hatty. So, at once, their play began
again in the garden, and went on as though the garden
and their games need never end.

They went tree climbing again—it was a passion with
them. As Hatty had mentioned not being able to climb
Tricksy, Tom taught her how to swarm. She did not
learn easily—chiefly from a horror of dirtying her clothes
so much that her aunt might notice and punish her; but
after a while she learnt how to wind her arms and legs
about the trunk, and worm her way upwards. In the end,
she climbed Tricksy: she was triumphant.

They played new games. Hatty found grasses of wild
barley growing in the wilderness, and picked them. She
showed Tom how to nip the top out of the grass-head
and then replace it; and, then, holding the grass in one
fist, she would knock against it with the other, repeating:
'Grandmother—Grandmother—jump out of bed'. On
the word 'jump', she would give a particularly hard
knock, and the top of the grass would spring out of
its green bed into the air and Hatty would laugh, and
Tom too.

Together they hunted for young frogs under the leaves
of the strawberry-bed ('Abel says they suck the straw-
berries') and set them hopping elsewhere; and once they
had the sight of a toad in a crevice under the threshold

stone of the greenhouse—like a stone himself, brown and dull and unmoving except for the breath in his sides.

They teased the birds of the garden—Tom was particularly good at surprising them, and at hoaxing the watchful jay; yet they protected them against all comers, too. Hatty let out birds from the gooseberry wire and from under the strawberry nets; and—when she was sure Abel was far away—she unlatched the door of his sparrow-trap. When any of the cousins came into the garden with a gun, Tom ran ahead, waving his arms and shouting, to warn the birds. Wild pigeons rose heavily from the rows of peas where they had been browsing, and made their way back to the safety of the wood. Nothing was ever shot—unless you could count Tom himself, who once received a spatter of pellets through his middle. Hatty went pale; but Tom laughed—they tickled him.

One day, when Tom and Hatty had been gazing at the sundial on the south wall, trying to make out how it told the time, they saw a wren light on one of the stone sunbeams above the dial, and then—the beams projected a little way away from the wall—disappear behind them.

'Do you think there's a wren's nest there?' whispered Hatty; and Tom thought there well might be; but, of course, one couldn't be sure from the path below.

'James once walked along the top of the sundial wall,' said Hatty.

'Well, I'm not going to,' said Tom. 'It would be just silly, not brave. That wall's far too high, and it'll be very narrow along the top: it would be far too dangerous.'

'Oh, Tom, I didn't mean that you should walk it!' said

Hatty, in dismay. 'James only did it for a dare. Cousin Edgar dared him, and James did it. He walked the whole length, and then he climbed down, and then he fought Cousin Edgar, and then he was sick. And Cousin Hubert heard about it all afterwards and was very angry, because he said James might have fallen and broken his neck.'

Tom was silent, turning over in his mind what Hatty had just said. He was beginning to change his mind about climbing the wall, because he saw that there could not be —for him—the danger that there had been for James. He might possibly fall off the wall, but a fall, even from such a height, could neither bruise nor break *him*.

He said to Hatty, 'I'm going to see if there really is a nest behind the sundial; I'm going to walk along that wall.'

'Oh, Tom!'

The way in which Hatty said, 'Oh, Tom!' made Tom feel warm and kind. He patted her hand. 'Don't worry. It's all right for me.'

He climbed, by means of the laddering branches of an espalier pear, to the top of the wall. In spite of all he had told himself, he felt a pang of horror when he stood upright upon it. The wall top was so narrow—nine inches, in some places weathered away to even less by the crumbling of brickwork; quite bushy plants grew along it, over which Tom would have to step; and on either side of that narrow, hazardous path the wall face went sheer and far: down to the orchard on one side; on the other, down to the garden, where Hatty stood, her pale face upturned to him. Tom knew, however, that he must not look down, if he were to keep his head and walk that wall top. He lifted his eyes and stepped resolutely forward.

Very soon he was over the porchway into the orchard, and then over the vine against the wall, and then over the sundial. He could see that dead leaves and other airy garden rubbish had drifted into the space between the stone sunbeams and the wall. At one end they seemed much denser than elsewhere: Tom got upon his hands and knees on the wall top and, peering closely, saw that this was indeed a wren's nest, with moss still greeny brown worked into it. He could see the little hole of entry.

'There is a wren's nest,' he called softly to Hatty. 'But I daren't touch it—I mean, I daren't for her sake.'

'Come back and come down now, Tom!'

He stood upright again, intending to turn back, as Hatty had said; but now, standing there, gazing freely about him, he was taken by a sudden joy. He began to pace along the wall like a king. Hatty was keeping step with him below, and whispering up to him; but he paid no attention, he was so far above her and the garden altogether. He had thought himself high when he had climbed to the top of the yew-trees, but he was higher now. In one sweep of the eye, he could see the whole lay-out of the garden, and the boundaries of walls and hedges that enclosed it. He could see the house: there was Susan leaning from an upper window to blow a kiss to somebody in the garden—Abel, he supposed. He could see into a courtyard of the house—a courtyard whose existence he had never suspected before: he saw Edgar there, engaged in washing Pincher in a tin bath of soapy water. Pincher looked very clean and wretched, with his neck poked forward and his ears back and his tail down. Tom, in exhilaration, called to him, 'Cheer up, Pincher!' Pincher heard him, or saw him, or even smelt him—it was difficult to tell which: even under the lather, his hackles rose, and he suddenly bolted from the bath, and had to be chased round the yard and caught by Edgar, who was very much annoyed and covered with splashes of soapsuds and water.

Tom saw beyond the garden and the house, to a lane, down which a horse and cart were plodding. Beyond the lane was a meadow, and then a meandering line that he knew must be the river. The river flowed past the meadow, and reached the village, and passed that. It reached a white handrailed bridge and slipped under it; and then away, towards what pools and watermills and locks and ferries that Hatty and Tom knew nothing of? So the river slipped away into the distance, in the direction of Castleford and Ely and King's Lynn, to the grandeur of the sea.

'What do you see beyond the garden, Tom?' Hatty whispered up to him, her curiosity having overcome her fears.

'If you were up here yourself to see . . .' Tom said; and his words floated high over the whole garden.

He could not tell her—could not hope to convey to her, without her seeing it, the distance. In a flat countryside— as this was—even a slight eminence gives a commanding view, as from a mountain peak. Tom, before, had known only the garden, and a very little beyond its limits; now, from his wall-top, he saw what seemed to be the whole world.

'Tell me what you see,' Hatty pleaded.

'Well, from the top of the wall you can see the river,' Tom began, 'and if you follow the river with your eye——'

'Yes? Yes?' whispered Hatty.

Tom did not finish what he was saying, for at that moment Abel came round the corner of the trees. He was running; he rushed straight at Hatty; he set his hands upon her shoulders and pressed down, so that Tom saw her suddenly crumple to the ground in a kneeling position. Then he thrust something into her hand, and, standing over her, began speaking in a lowered, quick voice. Tom heard Hatty's voice replying: she sounded frightened. He could not hear what either of them said.

In haste Tom retraced his steps along the wall and climbed down again into the garden. By that time, Hatty was alone.

'What on earth was the matter?' Tom asked.

'Abel thought I was going to walk along the top of the wall, as James did,' said Hatty. 'He wanted to stop me because of the danger.'

'I thought he was going to beat you.'

'He made me kneel down on the path and swear on his Bible—swear never to climb the sundial wall and walk along it.'

'Was he very angry?' asked Tom.

Hatty said slowly: 'No. I think—somehow—he was frightened.'

I

'Frightened?' Tom frowned. 'You mean that *you* were frightened; *he* was angry.'

'No. I was frightened a little, just because he was so quick and strong; but I'm sure he was frightened too, and much more frightened. When he made me take the Bible, his hand was all clammy and it shook.'

'Why did he suddenly think you might try to climb the wall?' asked Tom.

'Because he saw me looking up at it in that way, I suppose.'

'No, that couldn't be the reason,' said Tom. 'He was running when he came round the corner of the trees; he must have been running with his Bible in his hand before ever he came within sight of you.'

'Perhaps he heard me talking to you on the top of the wall.'

'No: you only whispered; and he couldn't have heard *me*.' By that Tom did not mean that he had spoken very quietly, for he had not; he meant that, even if he had shouted with all his strength, his voice could never have been heard by Abel.

'Well, then,' said Hatty, 'perhaps Susan saw me from a bedroom window, and came down and told him of it.'

'Perhaps,' said Tom. 'I saw Susan at a window.' But he was not satisfied with the explanation.

At about this time, Hatty and Tom started on the building of the tree-house, and they soon forgot Abel's strange behaviour in their absorption in the work.

XVI

The Tree-House

IN a letter to his brother, Tom wrote: '. . . I am glad your measles are over. I wish you were here. We are building a tree-house in the Steps of St Paul's.' Peter read the letter, and then burnt it, as he must burn all Tom's correspondence now. He went sombrely out into the Longs' little back-garden and began to put in some half-hearted work at a construction in the apple-tree.

Mrs Long, watching from the kitchen-window, called: 'I wish Tom were home to help you.' She spoke uneasily.

She had told herself again and again that she completely trusted Gwen and Alan with the boy; and indeed she did. Nevertheless, she sensed something unusual and mysterious in the air, and it troubled her.

The Kitsons were better off than the Longs—there is all the difference, in expense, between having two children and having none at all. Tom might have been made discontented with his home by the luxury he was experiencing away from it; but he was not—Mrs Long had to admit that. Tom's letters to his parents contained nothing but brief, dry reports of a dull life spent almost entirely in the company of his aunt and uncle. He did not seem to find any pleasure in it—not even in the meals, now. Yet he had asked more than once to be allowed to stay on.

'There are no other children there,' Mrs Long pointed out to her husband that evening; 'and Tom never seems to go anywhere very special. Does he tell you more, Peter, in his letters to you? They seem long enough.'

Peter looked at the ground. 'I think he just likes staying in that flat.'

'Well, he'll get out of mooning about indoors alone, when he comes home,' said Mr Long cheerfully. 'Won't he, Peter?'

'I suppose he'll have to come home for school, anyway,' said Peter. 'He missed the end of the summer term because of my measles, but he'll have to be home when school starts again.'

'When the autumn term starts!' cried Mrs Long in alarm. 'Why, we must have him home before that,

Peter!' Peter looked doubtful, so Mrs Long said: 'You surely don't want to spend all this summer without Tom?'

'I suppose —' said Peter, and waited for them to ask him what he supposed.

'Well?'

'I suppose that, if Tom doesn't want to come away from Aunt Gwen's yet, I couldn't go there too, and stay there with him . . .'

Mrs Long stared at her son, almost frightened; but Mr Long laughed: 'What on earth would *two* boys do in a poky flat without a garden?'

'I'd like to be there with Tom,' said Peter, stubbornly.

'You surely mean,' said his father, 'that you'd like to be *here* with Tom. You want him to come home.'

'You can't really want to go and stay with him in that flat,' said his mother.

'I do then!' said Peter. 'I do! I lie awake at night and wish I were there; and then I fall asleep and dream that I am there. I want to go—I do! I do!'

'But why, Peter, why?' asked his mother. Peter only cast his eyes down and repeated in a flat, obstinate voice that he knew that he would like it.

There the conversation was left, without conclusion. That night Mrs Long crept upstairs to the room that Peter shared with Tom. The door was ajar as usual, and she looked in: Peter was still awake. By the light of the street-lamp outside she could see that his eyes were open, staring across the room at the picture-postcard from Tom, that he had propped up on the mantelpiece. Mrs Long stole away, but came again later, and again. On the third

occasion, Peter was asleep. She went right into the bedroom and stood over him, looking down at him. He must
have been dreaming of something, for the expression on
his face changed a little, even in sleep. Once he smiled,
and then sighed; and once such a far-away look came into
his face that his mother bent over him in an impulse to
wake him and recall him to her. She restrained herself,
and left him.

On her way downstairs from the bedroom, Mrs Long
passed the tiny landing-window that looked over the
back-garden: she saw black projections from the apple-
tree there—the timbers of Peter's tree-house. His construction was certainly not as advanced as the one in the
Steps of St Paul's—although Mrs Long, of course, was
not in a position to make that comparison. Tom's tree-
house, anyway, already had the start of Peter's—a start
by as long as it takes for a letter to be written, delivered,
read and then burnt.

'Hatty works very hard at the tree-house', Tom had
written to Peter. 'She likes the idea of it.' There he
understated her feelings: Hatty was deeply excited about
the tree-house, to a degree that quite surprised Tom. For
one thing, she thought of it as her house in a way the big
house was not: that was her aunt's house, and her cousins',
and she was there only on sufferance. This tree-house,
however, could be her own house and home, and she
talked wildly of furnishing it with her doll's tea-set and
even with objects filched from the spare bedrooms of the
big house. Tom, in alarm, had to reason her into some
sense.

Then, again, Hatty loved the tree-house because it was the best of all her hiding-places in the garden. 'Nobody would ever suspect it was here,' she said, 'unless they had seen it being built. None of the cousins know.'

'Has Abel seen it?' asked Tom.

'He's never seen me carrying stuff or climbing up or even coming in this direction. I've been very careful to keep out of his sight.'

'I haven't bothered about that,' said Tom; 'but, of course, he's never seen me, anyway.'

'Of course not,' agreed Hatty; and then they changed the subject hurriedly, for their quarrel about ghosts and which of them was one was still fresh in their minds.

However, as it turned out, Abel certainly must have known about the tree-house.

That afternoon he was working in the garden, netting the strawberry beds: Hatty and Tom knew that, because they always liked to locate Abel and anybody else in the garden, before they went up into their tree-house. This time they made sure that only Abel was about, and that he was some way away. Then they climbed up.

By now, the house was finished, but Hatty still had ambitions. 'If it's to be anything like a real house,' she said, 'it should have windows—not just accidental gaps in the walls.' The windows must be oblong in shape, Hatty said, like those of the big house.

'You're expecting too much,' Tom grumbled; and in the end Hatty herself had to make the windows—such as they were. There were two of them.

They were still more like ragged holes than windows.

Hatty worked patiently from the inside and then from the outside, plaiting twigs along the window-edges, trying to make them straight and firm.

Tom was not helping. He hoped that Hatty would tire of the idea of house-windows and a house—although that did not seem likely at present. Then he would suggest a more interesting possibility: that the windows, after all, were portholes, and that this was the captain's cabin on a ship at sea.

Hatty never finished her windows. She was humming as she moved from one bough to another outside the wall of the tree-house; then she stopped to call to Tom: 'Tom, there's a cracked bough this side—is it all right? Have you ever sat on it?'

'A cracked bough?' said Tom. 'Oh, yes, I've been out on that one.' Hatty's humming was resumed, jerkily, as she began to move again. 'Only,' Tom began to add, 'I daresay I'm different: I wouldn't advise *you*——'

He did not see it happen, but the cracked bough must have begun to break at once, even at the first pressure of Hatty's slight weight. He heard the cracking, tearing sound; he heard Hatty's little 'Oh!' of surprise that lasted only a part of a second before it became a scream, as she felt herself falling.

Hatty's cry was a thin, high one that pierced through all the garden. Birds rose and scattered at the sound; a red squirrel that was running along the nut stub tops froze to a branch; and Abel—Abel flung down his armful of strawberry net and began running in the direction of the Steps of St Paul's.

Tom had jumped the whole height of the tree and had landed—more weightless than a cat—beside Hatty. She lay on the ground, dumb now, and still: her body was curved round, and—in falling—her pinafore had been flung up so that now it partly covered her face. Where the fabric touched her forehead, there was a bloodstain that crept along the fibres.

Tom was still standing helplessly beside her, when Abel thudded up. Abel saw the blood and groaned aloud; he picked Hatty up in his arms and began to carry her towards the house. Tom went with them.

Then Abel stopped suddenly. He half-turned round, so that he faced the spot where Tom was. Through all the numbness of his horror at what had happened, Tom realized that Abel was looking at him, not through him; and now he was beginning to speak to him. 'Get you gone!' said Abel, hoarsely.

Tom stared back at him; neither of them budged.

'Get you back to Hell, where you come from! I know you. I've seen you always, and thought best not to see you; and heard you and thought best to seem deaf; but I've known you, and known you for what you are!'

Tom ignored all, except that Abel could hear him and therefore could answer him. 'Oh!' he cried, 'do you know —is Hatty alive, or is she dead?'

'Aye,' said Abel, 'you've tried to kill her often enough— her that had neither mother nor father nor home here— nothing but her innocence, against your devilry with bow and arrows and knives and high places. Now, I say, get you gone!'

Tom did not go; but Abel, still carrying Hatty, began to back away, across the lawn and towards the house. As he went, he repeated in a loud voice that prayer which Tom had thought to be only a grace after meat: '. . . May the Lord keep me from all the works of the Devil, that he hurt me not.' Abel's voice shook; and he stumbled with his burden as he felt his way ever backwards, with his eyes fixed upon Tom, up the garden doorstep, and through the garden door. The garden door was slammed, and Tom heard the sound of the bolt going home.

Then Tom woke from amazement. He ran forward to the door and flung himself upon it, wildly beating his fist on the wood, and calling first upon Abel to let him in, and then upon Hatty. The door remained shut; his crying and knocking brought no one. Of those that might have heard him and let him in, it seemed that one would not, and the other could not.

XVII

In Search of Hatty

A<small>T</small> the end of his first frenzy of battery upon the out-side of the garden door, Tom leaned against it, sobbing for breath. From inside he heard the grandfather clock coolly striking the hour, and a distant upstairs noise of voices and hurried feet.

He could not open the door, and, he now realized, he had exhausted the strength of body and will that might have carried him through it. He was shut out from Hatty; and he was also shut out from his own bed in the Kitsons' flat. But the fear for Hatty remained greater than the fear for himself.

Tom withdrew across the lawn into one of the yew-alcoves. All he could do was wait.

It seemed a long time before the garden door opened and Abel walked out. Tom went across to him at once, and addressed him: 'Abel, please, how is Hatty?'

Tom thought that he had prepared himself for anything from Abel: if Abel believed him to be a demon from Hell, disguised as a boy and intent upon bringing misfortune to Hatty—if he believed that, then he would hate Tom and rail against him, cursing him and banning him with exorcism of prayers and the Bible. The one thing that Tom had not been prepared for was that Abel should go back to his safeguard of refusing to see or hear Tom at all.

'Abel—Abel—Abel,' Tom begged, 'she's not dead, is she? She's not dead?' At last he saw Abel's eyelids flicker, and that for a moment he allowed himself to see Tom. Tom's face had the dirt of tree-climbing upon it, and two clean tracks through the dirt, from eyes to chin, where tears of exhaustion and terror had made their way. Altogether, there was about Tom something so like a boy and so unlike a demon that Abel was trapped, for the last time, into speaking directly to him.

'No,' said Abel, 'she's alive'; and he fixed his eyes straight ahead again, took a deep breath, and walked deliberately through the side of Tom's body and on towards the potting-shed.

Abel had left the garden door open behind him—as it always stood in these days of summer. Tom's thought was at once to go into the house again, though whether to get himself to bed or to find out more about Hatty, he did not think out.

The matter was settled for him. This time, the furniture did not dissolve in front of him as he advanced up the hall: the stuffed creatures held their ground, and stared at him firmly with their glass eyes through the glass sides of their cases; he had time to notice the mercury in the barometer and to see that it reached to Very Dry. He saw everything, clear and solid, as he passed it. He came to the grandfather clock; he saw that its fingers were pointing to eleven minutes to five, and saw again the design behind the fingers. Even in his anxiety for Hatty, his attention was arrested by it: there was nothing new to be seen, and yet he seemed to be seeing everything freshly. He still did not know who or what was the angel creature painted there, striding on sea and land, with open book; but he felt that he almost knew the meaning; one day, soon, he might know.

Now he turned from the grandfather clock and towards the staircase: he saw it carpeted. Each carpet-tread was held in place by a shining brass rod, and, tread by tread, the carpet mounted softly and steadily upstairs.

Tom took a step towards the staircase and then halted, wondering at what he was about to do. Behind him he was leaving that garden-kingdom of Hatty's where he and Hatty and Abel were the only three inhabitants— and Abel had even denied that there were more than two.

He was leaving that and going forward into the Melbournes' house: already the Melbournes and their lives
seemed to be pressing round upon him. At the foot of the
stairs, to the right, was a row of pegs from which hung
Melbourne hats and caps and coats and capes. Next to
these was a boot cupboard: Tom knew it was a boot cupboard because the door was ajar and he could see the shelves
inside, and, standing upon them, all the Melbourne boots
and shoes and slippers and pumps and gaiters and waders
and spats. Opposite the coat-pegs, on Tom's left, was
another of the brackets, and on it had been left two
marbly-backed ledgers and a little safety inkwell and an
old-fashioned round ruler of ebony: which Melbourne did
they belong to? There was a door next to the bracket—
the door through which Susan had once come with her
kindling wood and matches; now, from the other side of
it, Tom heard a murmur of women's voices. He couldn't
hear what they were saying; he couldn't hear who they
were, although he imagined that one voice sounded like
Susan's.

Tom felt among many strangers, and lonely. There was
no Hatty here, and his secret fear was that there might be
no Hatty anywhere. Abel had said: 'She's alive'; but
perhaps that meant, 'She's just alive', or even, 'She's alive,
but can't live long.' In the past Tom had managed to
convince himself that Hatty was a ghost, and now he must
face what went with that: that, at some time, she must
have died. Ghosts had always died before they became so
—Tom's reasoning ran in anxious, confused circles.

He needed a great deal of courage to go forward and

set his foot on the bottom step of that soft, silent stair. Perhaps—although Tom could be very brave—perhaps he would have lacked the last touch of courage, but for the sound of the grandfather clock behind him. Its ticking sounded to him like a human heart, alive and beating—and he thought of Hatty when he thought that. He braced himself and began going upstairs.

When he reached the upstairs landing he was in a part of the Melbournes' house that he had never seen before. So it seemed to Tom: he had forgotten that this house was, too, the house in which, somehow, his aunt and uncle, as well as other tenants, lived. There was not very much to remind him of that now. The first-floor landing of the Melbournes' house was carpeted, and wider than the corridor between the flats that Tom knew, and there were many doors off it, each leading to a bedroom, instead of two doors only, which were the front doors of two flats. The little stairway that had simply gone up to Mrs Bartholomew's front door now ended in a tiny landing with three doors off it.

Tom surveyed the first landing: every door was shut. So were the three doors on the attic floor. Behind which of all these doors did Hatty lie?

There was really no clue, so Tom chose the nearest door on the first landing, took a deep breath, concentrated, tensed his muscles, and drove his head steadily through the woodwork and into the room on the other side.

Hatty was not in this bedroom. The dustsheets over the bed and over the other furniture showed it to be a spare room. Its window looked over the garden: Tom could see, even from his position in the door, the tops of the yew-trees opposite, and the great height of the ivied fir, unfallen. He was looking only for Hatty, so he did not linger over this view, but later he had cause to remember it.

He wrenched his head back through the door again, and considered what next to do. He had intended to push his head through each door in turn, until he found Hatty; but now he wondered whether that method would be wise. Already he was tiring; and his ears were singing and his eyes aching, and even his stomach, which had remained on the safe side of the door, was heaving a little. If Hatty were behind the last door he came to try, he might never be able to reach her.

Surely, in these special circumstances, dishonest methods were excusable. Tom began to peep through keyholes, and to listen at them. Through the third keyhole he heard something: a very soft, rhythmic swishing sound. He could not think what made it, and the keyhole-view showed him only a washstand with basin and ewer, a length of lace curtain draped over part of a window, and a very upright chair.

No, he could not imagine what the noise could be; surely, at least, it could not be coming from Hatty lying ill, perhaps dying. The thought of her thus made him turn desperately on to try the other doors; and then, again, even as he turned, he thought that perhaps Hatty was lying in that room, after all, but delirious, no sound or motion except for her hands that ceaselessly and softly stroked down the sheet of her bed: swish—swish—swish.

Tom turned back to the door from behind which that sound came and began fairly to ram his head through it. He was up to his eyebrows in the woodwork when he heard—his ears were still free—a step on the stairs behind him. Tom had a horror of being caught part-way through a door: he pulled back and faced about quickly.

A man was coming upstairs. He carried under one arm the office-ledgers that Tom had noticed in the hall below; he held the inkwell and ruler in his hand. He had the grave look of someone who earns his living and has just finished earning it for the day. Who was he? A Melbourne, Tom was sure: those were Melbourne features.

The man came directly along the landing—directly towards Tom; but he had no concern with Tom, after all. He stopped by the very door that Tom had been trying, and knocked gently.

'Mother?'

The swishing sound stopped. A voice that Tom recognized at once as Hatty's aunt's said: 'Who is that?'

'James.'

James? Tom was startled: James had only been a youth when Tom had last seen him, in the garden. Had so much of Melbourne time passed in so little of Tom's time, that James had grown into a man—and a business man at that? Here he certainly was, broad and tall and strong, with a high, shiny collar, and that face of gravity above it.

'You can come in,' said the woman's voice. 'I'm only brushing my hair.'

James went in, and Tom went with him. He had not meant to, for he was not an inquisitive, impertinent boy,

K

but James's question, even as he opened the door, was: 'How is Hatty?'

They both stood inside the bedroom door: the man and the boy. Once James looked round him uneasily, as people will who know they are alone and yet guess at some other presence in the room—a cat's perhaps.

In front of her dressing-table mirror stood Hatty's aunt. Her long brown hair fell heavily as low as to her waist, and she was passing her hairbrush down it, from scalp to tips, with that steady, swishing sound. Tom saw, as he watched, that the hair was not all brown now, but greying: time had passed, too, for Hatty's aunt.

She was not answering James at once. She stopped brushing her hair and began twisting it and braiding it. As she did so, she said, casually and coldly, 'Hatty will do well enough.'

'Is that what the doctor says?'

'Yes.'

'We must be thankful, then.'

'Thankful!' With her hands still at her hair, Hatty's aunt turned to face her son. 'Thankful! But what was she doing, to have the accident? Climbing trees, if you please! Has she no sense of what is fitting to her sex and to her age now? She is old enough to know better!'

'Hatty is young for her age,' said James. 'Perhaps it comes from her being by herself so much—playing alone —always in the garden.'

'Oh, you were always kind to her!' cried Hatty's aunt, and she made what she said sound like a bitter accusation. 'And so she is never to grow up! What is to happen to

her, if so? I don't know. She is a strange enough girl as
it is.' Hatty's aunt had turned back to the mirror to arrange
the braidings of her hair.

'Of course Hatty will grow up,' said James, and Tom
admired the way in which he stood up to his mother's
anger. 'But what is to become of her *then*?'

'She is not to expect anything more from me, surely.
I have given her charity enough.'

'In that case, Mother, she will have to earn her own living, somehow, although how she is to do that I don't know.
Or perhaps she will marry—although, again, she knows no
one and meets no one outside this house and garden.'

'I will not have her ruling in this house when I am gone.'
Hatty's aunt had not turned from the mirror, but was
staring intently into it at the image of her son reflected
there.

'What do you mean, Mother?'

'You and Hubert and Edgar are all grown now, and in
your father's business, and independent as far as that goes.
Very well; but if any of you thinks later of marrying
Harriet, do not expect ever to have a penny from me.
Hubert has never cared for the girl, and I believe Edgar
dislikes her; but you have pitied her.'

In the silence after this, Tom rather expected James,
who was so bold, to cry out that he had not thought before
of marrying Hatty, but now he saw what a good idea it
was, and he certainly would marry her as soon as she
was of age, and they would be rich and live happily
ever after—all in spite of his mother. But James was not
romantic. He gave a little sigh: 'I have had no intention of

ever marrying Hatty; I don't suppose that I ever shall have; but she is certainly to be pitied.'

'She is pitiable, certainly,' said Hatty's aunt, grimly.

'And surely, Mother, now she is growing up, she should see more of the world than this house and this garden can show her. She should meet more people; she should make acquaintances; she should make friends.'

'You know perfectly well that she loves only to be alone in the garden.'

'We can draw her from that. We have friends, and she must not be allowed always to hide away from them, as if she were afraid. When we make parties up she can be made to want to join them: boating on the river, and picnics; cricket matches to watch; whist-drives; carol singing at Christmas; skating . . .'

'She doesn't want to grow up; she wants only her garden.'

'We could make her want more. I'll go to her now, and talk to her and say that, when she is quite well again, she must go in for a gayer life. I'll say that we all want her to go out, to make friends.'

We all? Tom, watching the woman's face in the glass, saw a cold disagreement in it.

'Can I say that you wish it, Mother?'

'You will waste your pity and your breath with Harriet.'

'Can I at least say that you agree?'

'You can say what you like to her; you can do what you like with her; and the less I see of her, the better.'

She turned her head, so that she saw her son neither in

reflection nor in the flesh. James withdrew, and Tom with him. James went to a door at the end of the landing, knocked softly and entered.

Tom waited outside, until the interview with Hatty should be over. He listened to the rise and fall of James's voice as he talked. He spoke gently, as though to someone who was ill, or had been so; but he spoke at great length, and Tom thought that Hatty's injury could not have been as serious as he had feared, if she could listen to all that James had to tell her.

XVIII

The Bedroom with Two Barred Windows

JAMES came out at last, shut Hatty's door behind him and went along the landing to what must be his own room. Tom waited until he heard that door open and shut again. Then he set himself against Hatty's bedroom door and began pressing his way through.

When Hatty saw him coming, she cried out in delight. 'But, please, Tom—please come through slowly—I want to see how it's done!'

'It's a knack,' said Tom; but he obligingly slowed up

his progress and made a very leisurely arrival on to the carpet of Hatty's bedroom. He felt the better for it.

Hatty was sitting up in bed, with a bandage round her head. Her face was flushed with excitement, but not with fever.

'Oh, I wish I could do that!' she sighed at Tom, and sank back among her pillows. Tom studied her for a moment: perhaps—no, *certainly*, she looked older than when he had first known her. Hatty had been growing up, just like the other Melbournes, and Tom had never noticed it, partly because they had been together so much and partly because he was not observant of such things.

'Well, how are you?' Tom asked. It would have been rude to stare longer.

'Very well,' said Hatty; 'and the doctor says the scar won't show. And Cousin James has visited me, and he says I must do other things besides falling out of trees, in the future.'

'Things without me?' said Tom, thinking of the grown-up parties of which James had spoken.

'Oh, no, Tom, whenever you want to come, so you shall!' But Tom noticed that she spoke to him as if he were a child and she were not.

'Sit down and talk to me, Tom,' she begged him.

He sat down on the end of the bed, and looked round the room. 'You've a nice bedroom.' It was a spacious room—as were all the rooms in the Melbournes' handsome house. It had a large cupboard, and two large windows, between which Hatty's bed stood; and across the bottom of the windows——

'You've bars across the bottom of your windows,' said Tom, 'as if this were a nursery.' And somewhere in his head the words seemed an echo of something he had once heard or said; and, indeed, the bars across the windows were like a remembrance of something once seen.

'It was a nursery,' said Hatty. 'My cousins' nursery, when they were little; and after that my nursery. And, then, because I was the last child, it just stayed my room. Now it's my bedroom.'

Tom stared at the windows as if he were mesmerized: he was remembering that he had seen them, or rather one of them—or, rather, again, each, but each separately, never together.

'Where is the bathroom in this house?' asked Tom.

'Bathroom?'

'Where do you have your bath?'

'I have my bath here in my bedroom, of course; the boys do in their rooms.'

'Here?' said Tom, staring round. 'How?'

'Why, there's the tin bath and Susan carries cans of hot water up from the kitchen. In winter there's a fire lit here, and I have my bath by the fire.'

'You could make a proper bathroom here,' said Tom, as though he saw it already done. 'You could run a partition somewhere down the middle of this room, here, so that there'd be a window on either side of the partition. Then this part of the room could still be a bedroom, and the room on the other side could be a bathroom.'

Hatty thought this an unnecessary and stupid idea, and

said so. 'Besides, this would only be a slice of a room, then.'

'Yes,' Tom agreed; 'and the partition will be—would be thin, and you'd always be able to hear the bath-water next door, as you lay here in bed.'

'I'd never want to hear that,' Hatty said positively.

'I don't suppose you ever will,' said Tom. 'Other people may.'

He moved over to the window and looked out. His gaze travelled far: first of all, over a lawn, at one end of which a giant beech-tree leaned in thought; over a hedge; a lane, another hedge; a meadow, with a great elm in the middle . . .

Tom took a deep breath: 'I like your room better,' he said, 'and I like your view much better.'

'And can you see the river beyond the meadow?' asked Hatty. 'But better than what, Tom?'

'Better—better than if there were nothing but houses opposite.'

Hatty laughed. 'Don't be silly, Tom! If that were so, we shouldn't be living on the edge of a village, as we do, but in a town.'

'Or in a village grown so big that it's really a town.' He seemed to change the subject. 'How many baths do you have, Hatty?'

'One a week. How many do you?

'One every other night. But I think I'd rather have fewer, and have this room and this view.'

Hatty looked at him, puzzled: she could not understand the connexion of his thoughts, nor understand a sadness that seemed to have come over him. 'Tom, there's nothing to be sad about.'

Tom was thinking about the Past, that Time made so far away. Time had taken this Present of Hatty's and turned it into his Past. Yet even so, here and now, for a little while, this was somehow made *his* Present too—his and Hatty's. Then he remembered the grandfather clock, that measured out both his time and Hatty's, and he remembered the picture on the face.

'Hatty, what does the picture on the grandfather clock mean?'

'It's something from the Bible.'

He was surprised. 'What?'

Hatty drew her brows together. 'It's difficult: I can't remember it—I mean, it's difficult to understand, so I can't remember it exactly. I'll find out, if you want to know.'

'Yes, please. Whom will you ask?'

Hatty smiled, but made no mystery of it, as an earlier Hatty might have done. 'I shall ask the clock; it's written there.'

'Where? I've never seen it.'

'No, you can't, because it's written so low down on the clock-face that the writing is hidden by the frame of the dial glass. You have to open the dial door to read it.'

'From inside the pendulum case, by a catch?'

'Yes, but how did you know?'

'Never mind. Who keeps the key to the pendulum-case?'

She smiled again. 'The grandfather clock. The key is always in the keyhole.'

Tom was shocked. 'But anyone might unlock it!'

'Only Aunt needs to, to wind the clock; she has forbidden anyone else to touch it.'

'But if strangers came to the house. Inquisitive people? Boys?'

Hatty simply did not understand him. She promised, however, that when she was next downstairs, and if there were nobody about, she would unlock the pendulum-case and unlatch the dial-door: then Tom could read the secret for himself.

There was nothing more that could be done now, so the subject was changed. Hatty took over the conversation, as Tom seemed thoughtful and quiet; she entertained him with tales of the nursery bedroom. Of how, behind the slatted shutters of these front windows of the house, bats slept in the daytime—you could fold back the shutters and see them hanging there, black among the grey cobwebs and dried wistaria leaves and dust; and how, one night, one had come into her room by mistake and swooped around it like a tiny black spectre, and she had screamed and screamed from under the sheet, because Susan had told her that bats made for long hair and entangled themselves in it, and then all your hair had to be cut off. (Tom smiled, and even Hatty smiled a little.) Then there had been the summer when a wistaria tendril had come in at the top of the window and twined itself the whole length of the bell-wire before Hatty's aunt had seen it and ordered it to be cut; and when you lay still you could hear mice running races behind the skirting-boards, and there were always more mice after the harvest, in the autumn, because they came in from the fields then. And then, of course, there was the cupboard——

At this point, Hatty jumped out of bed to show Tom the cupboard—not her clothes hanging there, but a secret hiding-place she had had, since she was a child, under the floorboards. She scrabbled with her finger-nails and levered up a section of floorboard, and there below, in a roomy space between the joists, was her little hoard: her one-bladed Fair knife, and a box of paints, and a small, pale-brown picture of a solemn-looking young gentleman leaning against an armchair in which sat a young woman. 'That was my mother and father, long ago. You remember, Tom, I once used to pretend to you that they were a King and Queen.'

Then Hatty had to get quickly back into bed again, for they heard footsteps along the landing outside. Summer dusk had begun shadowing the room, and now Susan arrived with an oil-lamp which she put on the mantelshelf and lit. Then she went away and came back again with a bowl of bread-and-milk for Hatty's supper.

While Hatty ate, Tom and she talked on, and Tom warmed his fingers over the opening of the lamp-glass and watched the shadow patterns his fingers made on the ceiling. From downstairs sounded the reverberation of the gong, calling the Melbournes to their evening meal; they heard footsteps and voices going downstairs.

Susan came again and took away the empty bowl and the lamp, and bade Hatty lie down and go to sleep. When Susan had gone, Tom said that he had better be going too.

'Very well,' said Hatty. She never asked where he would go.

'I shall see you tomorrow,' said Tom.

Hatty smiled. 'You always say that, and then it's often months and months before you come again.'   Que.

'I come every night,' said Tom.

He said good night to her, and went downstairs. In the hall there was a smell of food, and Susan and another maid were running to and fro with plates and dishes: the family was dining.

Tom paused to check that the key of the grandfather clock was in its keyhole. He longed to be able to turn it, but Hatty must do that for him. He stared at the angel on the clock-face.

He left the clock and went out into the garden, and then very deliberately came in again and—shutting his eyes—closed the door and bolted it. But when he opened his eyes again, the hall was still the Melbournes' hall. He went along it and upstairs, hoping desperately that, even as he went, the stair-carpet and rods would dissolve away beneath him, and he would find himself on the way to the Kitsons' flat and his own bedroom there and his own bed.

No such thing happened. He reached Hatty's bedroom, that should have been his; the door was ajar.

'Who's that?' Hatty mumbled sleepily.

'It's only me,' said Tom. 'I—I came back for something.'

'Have you got it?'

'No,' said Tom. 'But it's all right. Good night, Hatty.'

'Good night.'

He went downstairs and out into the garden, and walked

right round it, under the flickering bats; and then he tried again: the house was still the same—the Melbournes' house.

'I shall never get back,' Tom thought suddenly; and then, 'I'll tell Hatty. I'll ask her what to do. I'll tell her everything, even if it does mean talking about ghosts.'

He went upstairs and slid into the bedroom, and called Hatty's name into the darkness. She did not reply, and, when he listened, he heard the regular breathing of a sleeper. He did not like to waken her and frighten her, so he crouched down on the floor by the bed, with his arm across one of hers, so that when she woke or even stirred he would at once feel her movement. He let his head rest on his arm and gradually felt himself falling asleep.

He did not know how much later it was when he woke, except that there was daylight in the room, and he was cramped from his position on the floor. At first, he did not know where he was. Then he remembered sharply and clutched with his arm across the bed, but the bed was empty—no Hatty. Then he saw that the bed was his, not Hatty's, and that this, too, was his bedroom—only a slice of a room with one barred window.

Tom did not understand how he came to be there, but he was grateful with all his heart. He was about to climb into his cold bed, when he remembered the bedroom slipper that wedged the flat door open. It would never do for his aunt or uncle to find it there. Fortunately the hour was still too early for them to be awake. He got the slipper, shut the front door and went back to bed. There he lay, looking up at the ceiling, until he heard his uncle go into the bathroom on the other side of the flimsy partition and start the water running for an early bath.

A moment afterwards, his aunt came in to Tom, bringing the early cup of tea with which she spoiled him.

'It's time to get up, Tom. The post has just brought a letter from home—one for you from Peter, and one for me from your mother.'

XIX

Next Saturday

THEY all sat round the breakfast-table: Alan Kitson
with his newspaper; his wife with a long letter from
her sister, Tom's mother; Tom himself with a letter from
Peter. Tom read his letter with one hand curved round
the top, to prevent any—even accidental—overlooking.

'Dear Tom,

BEWARE! Mother is writing to Aunt Gwen to say
can you come home at the end of the week and this
time you really are to. I think Mother will say you
must come because I miss you so much but I don't
want you to come away. I like all you write in your
letters. Tell me some more. I wish I were there but
Mother and Father say no.

154

I wish we had more trees and a river near and a high wall. I *wish* I were there.

'Yours

'Pete.'

Tom sighed; he would have liked to bring Peter, if only for a little, to the reach of his wishes.

Tom looked back to the beginning of the letter: 'BEWARE!' But what can children do against their elders' decisions for them, and especially their parents'? 'You are to come home at the end of the week'; and this—Tom looked at the top of Uncle Alan's newspaper—this was Tuesday. He supposed that they would be suggesting Saturday or Sunday for his return.

Aunt Gwen put down her letter and smiled at Tom, but sadly. 'Well, Tom, so we must really say good-bye to you soon.'

'When?' said Tom, abruptly.

'On Saturday. There's a cheap train on Saturday morning, and your mother says you can go by train, now that you're out of quarantine.'

'Next Saturday?' said Tom. 'So soon?'

His uncle said suddenly: 'We shall miss you, Tom.' Then he looked surprised—almost annoyed—at what he had said.

Aunt Gwen said: 'Your father and mother send their special love, Tom, and look forward to seeing you again soon. Your mother says that Peter has been missing you very much; he pines and daydreams without you; he *needs* you. We could hardly expect to keep y⟨...⟩ here—unless we adopted you.'

L

If they adopted him, Tom thought, he could stay here; but, on the other hand, he wouldn't have his own family any more: his mother, his father, Peter . . .

Tom felt a tightness round his ribs, as though he were being squeezed apart there. He wanted two different sets of things so badly: he wanted his mother and father and Peter and home—he really did want them, badly; and, on the other hand, he wanted the garden.

'If you adopted me,' Tom began, slowly and painfully.

'I was only joking, Tom,' said his aunt, thinking to reassure him.

So she did, in part, for Tom had not at all wanted to become the Kitsons' child and to stop belonging to his own family; but, all the same, some desperate remedy must be found for his now desperate situation. He knew, from Peter's letter and from the way his aunt had spoken, that he had no further hope of prolonging his stay here—not by postponements, not by chills, not even by adoption. They had said Saturday morning, and that was that.

Next Saturday . . .

'Perhaps next year,' his aunt was saying, 'you'll come again and spend part of your summer holiday with us.'

Tom could not answer her and thank her, because next year was so far away, and the feeling round his heart, here and now, was so bad when he thought of going—so bad that one might have said his heart was nearly breaking.

All that morning, Tom seemed to hear the ticking of the grandfather clock, bringing Saturday, minute by minute, nearer and nearer. He hated the clock for that. Then he would remember that, this very night, the grandfather clock was to give up its secret, when Hatty unfastened the doors. What the secret might be, Tom could not even dimly guess; yet he had a strange feeling of its importance, and he found himself setting a faint hope upon it—his only hope. For that reason, he longed for the minutes and hours to pass quickly until tonight. Time was so long from now until then; so short from now until Saturday.

Que.

That afternoon, Tom wrote to Peter about the garden, with a hopefulness he did not really feel; he promised to write more tomorrow. Then, to get away from the ticking of the clock, he went out for a walk with his aunt. He had asked whether there was not a river flowing near by, and she had thought so and that she could find it for him. They walked among back streets, turning this way and that until Tom lost all sense of direction. They came to a bridge.

'Here's your river, Tom!' said Aunt Gwen, triumphantly.

It *must* be the same river, although it looked neither like the stretch Tom had glimpsed from Hatty's window nor like the one he and Hatty had reached through the meadow by the garden hedge. This river no longer flowed beside meadows: it had back-garden strips on one side and an asphalt path on the other.

There was a man fishing by the bridge, and Aunt Gwen called to him: 'Have you caught any fish?'

'There aren't any fish,' the man replied sourly. He stood by a notice that said: 'WARNING. The Council takes no responsibility for persons bathing, wading or paddling. These waters have been certified as unsuitable for such purposes, owing to pollution.'

'What is pollution?' Tom asked.

'I know it means that the river isn't pure and healthy any more,' said Aunt Gwen. 'It's something to do with all the houses that have been built, and the factories. Dreadful stuff gets into rivers from factories, I believe.'

Tom looked at the river-water: it did not look foul, but he saw that the weeds below the surface of the water, instead of being slim and green and shining, were clothed in a kind of dingy, brown fur. There were no geese about, nor any waterfowl. There certainly seemed to be no fish. On the other hand, there was a large quantity of broken glass, broken crockery and empty tins dimly to be seen on the river-bed.

'Can't you bathe or paddle anywhere?' asked Tom.

'There's bathing at Castleford. This river flows down to Castleford, you know.'

'To Castleford, Ely, King's Lynn and the sea,' said Tom.

'Why, yes, Tom,' said his aunt, rather surprised. 'How did you come to know that piece of geography?'

'Someone told me,' Tom said reservedly. 'What is the time, please?'

'Nearly four o'clock.'

Was that all?

They walked home again, there being nothing more of interest to see. As they came in through the front-door of the big house, the first thing Tom heard was the ticking of the grandfather clock. It would tick on to bedtime, and in that way Time was Tom's friend; but, after that, it would tick on to Saturday, and in that way Time was Tom's enemy.

XX

The Angel Speaks

THAT Tuesday night Tom did not know how he might
find Hatty—whether she would still be in bed after
her fall, or whether she would be up and about in the
garden again, or whether she would already be trying
out the social pleasures with which James had tempted her.

Tom had been ready for changes in Hatty; what took him utterly by surprise, when he opened the garden door, was a change in the season. It was mid-winter—not a dreary, grey mid-winter, but one shining with new-fallen snow. Every tree and bush and plant was muffled in white; only the deeper alcoves of the yews had been sheltered from snow, and these seemed to watch Tom like dark, deep-set eyes.

In its way, this weather was as perfect as the summer weather had been.

There was a great stillness; and Tom held his breath, enchanted by the scene before him. Then a moorhen—probably driven by the severity of the weather to leave the river and seek food in the garden—appeared from under one of the bushes by the lawn; stooping, nervously jerky, and yet unhurried, it trod its way lightly across the snow of the lawn and disappeared again under the shrubs.

The movement broke the spell for Tom. He looked around him and saw that there were other prints in the snow besides the moorhen's light, three-toed impressions. Human feet had walked out of the garden door, along the path, across a corner of the lawn and gone round by the greenhouse in the direction of the pond. Tom was at once sure that these were Hatty's, and he followed the trail.

Round the end of the greenhouse he tracked her, and then came within sight of the pond. There was Hatty. The pond was frozen over, and one end had been swept clear of snow: in this space Hatty was skating—if one could call it skating yet. She had one of the chairs from the summer-house and was pushing it before her, and striking out with her skates as she went, gasping aloud with the effort and concentration. Yet when Tom called her, she turned to him a face bright with joy.

'Why, Tom!' she cried, and hobbled towards the side of the pond, and stood there with her toes turned inwards as if otherwise her skates might take it into their heads to try dashing away in opposite directions.

'Hatty,' said Tom, 'I wanted you—you promised——'

'But you're thinner!' said Hatty, frowning to herself.

'Thinner?' said Tom, 'No, I'm fatter.' He knew that for certain, because Aunt Gwen had recently paid a penny to have him weighed, and she had been very pleased with the result.

'I didn't mean that; I meant thinner *through*,' said Hatty, and then said, with a look of consternation, 'Oh, no, I didn't mean that either—at least, I don't know what I could have meant, or rather——'

'It doesn't matter,' said Tom, impatiently; 'but I want you to find out for me about the picture on the grandfather clock.' He saw Hatty looking uncertain, so he added: 'You did say you would.'

'Did I?'

'When you fell from our tree-house. We talked of it after that.'

'Why, that was long ago! If you've waited so long, Tom, couldn't you wait a little longer? Must you know now? Wouldn't you rather watch me skate?' In a rush she told Tom how her skating was improving, and that soon she could go skating with the others—with Hubert and James and Edgar and Bertie Codling and the Chapman girls and young Barty and all the others. 'Don't you like skating, Tom?' she ended. 'Haven't you ever learnt?'

'Yes,' said Tom, 'but now, Hatty, please do as you promised, and come and open the grandfather clock for me and show me what the picture means!'

Sighing, Hatty sat down on the summer-house chair, took off her skating-boots and skates, put on her ordinary shoes, and went back with Tom to the house. As she went, she said something about the explanation of the picture being a revelation—or so Tom thought he heard her say.

In the hall, standing by the grandfather clock, Hatty listened carefully for a moment. 'Aunt will be upstairs.' She turned the key in the keyhole and unlocked the clock-case. While she was feeling for the catch to the dial-front, Tom took a look at the inside of the pendulum-case. He saw shadows and cobwebs; and then he saw the pendulum that swung to and fro with the ticking of the clock. The bob that ended the pendulum was a flat, round disc of metal, gilded: it shone like a sun as it moved to and fro. Tom saw that there was a flourish of lettering across the gilt; even as the bob swung, he could make out what was written there: 'Time No Longer.'

'Time no longer?' said Tom in surprise.

'Yes,' said Hatty, struggling with the unfamiliar latch. 'That's it.'

'But no longer than what?'

'No, no! You don't understand. Wait——'

She found the catch at last, and released it, and swung back the dial-door, and pointed out to Tom the writing, very low down, well below the wide-apart feet of the angel with his book. 'Look! I thought it was the Book of Revelation; but I couldn't remember the chapter and verse.'

Tom read: 'Rev. x. 1–6.' He was repeating this aloud, to memorize it, when Hatty said, 'Hush! Wasn't that a movement upstairs?' In a fright, she re-fastened the clock-doors, and hurried Tom away into the garden.

'Revelation chapter ten verses one to six,' Tom repeated as they went.

'I ought to get my Bible and then I could look it up for you,' said Hatty; but she seemed very much disinclined to go indoors again and upstairs.

Then Tom thought of Abel's Bible, that he kept in the heating-house; and they went there. Tom noticed how easily Hatty opened the door, now: she reached the square of iron at the top, without even needing to stand on her toes. She had certainly grown a great deal since those early days in the garden.

The inside of the heating-house looked quite different in winter-time. The furnace was working to heat the water for the greenhouse pipes, and the little place was stuffily warm and glowing with light. Hatty found the Bible easily and brought it out to Tom.

She began to turn the pages towards the end of the volume, muttering to herself: '—Titus—Philemon—'Pistle-to-the-Hebrews—'Pistle-to-James—First-of-Peter—Second-of-Peter—First-of-John—Second-of-John—Third-of-John—Jude—REVELATION. Revelation is the last book in the Bible.'

Hatty was now among the chapters of the Revelation of

St John the Divine, and Tom was reading over her arm. There was the slightest sound—the sound of snow being compressed under a footfall—and they both looked up: Abel had come round the corner of the nut stubs. Perhaps he had been on his way to stoke the furnace; perhaps—for he carried a besom broom—he had come to sweep the rest of the pond-ice for Hatty.

He stood dumbfounded.

Hatty saw the amazement on Abel's face, and misunderstood it: she thought he was looking at the Bible, whereas he was looking at Tom—or rather, at Tom in the company of the Bible. 'Abel,' said Hatty nervously, 'do you mind? We—I mean, I, of course—I wanted to look something up in the Bible, quickly.'

Abel still stared.

'I'm very sorry if you object,' said Hatty, and waited.

'No . . . No . . .' He seemed to be working something out in his mind. 'For there's Truth in that Book, and Salvation. Them that reads in that Book—no, they cannot be altogether damned.' He touched his forelock, in what seemed a kind of misplaced apology, but Tom knew that the apology was intended and was for him. With that, as though he did not like to intrude, Abel left them.

They went back to their search in the Bible; and now Hatty had found the right chapter and the right verses:

'And I saw another mighty angel come down from heaven, clothed with a cloud: and a rainbow was upon his head, and his face was as it were the sun, and his feet as pillars of fire: and he had in his hand a little book open: and he set his right foot upon the sea, and his left foot on the earth, and cried with a loud voice, as when a lion roareth: and when he had cried, seven thunders uttered their voices. And when the seven thunders had uttered their voices, I was about to write: and I heard a voice from heaven saying unto me,

'"Seal up those things which the seven thunders uttered, and write them not."

'And the angel which I saw stand upon the sea and upon the earth lifted up his hand to heaven, and sware by him that liveth for ever and ever, who created heaven, and the things that therein are, and the earth, and the things that therein are, and the sea, and the things which are therein, that there should be time no longer.

Tom's head, when he had finished reading, whirled with cloud and rainbow and fire and thunder and the majesty of it all—perhaps like the head of the unknown dial-painter of long ago.

Tom did not understand, however, and he said so.

'It's difficult,' Hatty agreed. 'I don't think anyone knows for certain what it all means. The Book of Revelation is full of angels and beasts and strange sayings. It's like that.'

'But the end of it—"time no longer"—what does that mean?' Tom insisted. 'I must know: it's important—it's written on the pendulum of the clock, and the angel swore it—swore that there should be time no longer. What did he mean?'

'Perhaps when the Last Trump sounds—when the end of

the world comes,' said Hatty, vaguely; and Tom could see that she was going to be of no more help to him. Already she had shut the Bible and had taken a step backwards, to return it to the heating-house. Her eyes had gone to the pond and they brightened—yes, Abel was sweeping the rest of the ice for her.

'Time no longer . . .' murmured Tom, and thought of all the clocks in the world stopping ticking, and their striking stopped too, drowned and stopped for ever by the sound of a great Trumpet. 'Time no longer . . .' repeated Tom; and the three words began to seem full of enormous possibilities.

Hatty had replaced the Bible. 'Are you coming to the pond with me, Tom, to watch me skate?'

'No,' said Tom. 'I must think.'

Already wrapped in thought, he turned from her and from all the frosty-sparkling distractions of the garden he loved so well, and went indoors and upstairs to bed.

XXI

Time and Time Again

FOR the rest of Tuesday night Tom lay in bed, at first thinking, and then, at last, dreaming—but of the same things, and of other things that floated up from the bottom of his mind and joined them. He dreamed that it was his last night here. He went downstairs to go into the garden; but he found that the angel had come down from the clock-face and—grown to giant-size—barred the way with a flaming sword. Yet Tom would not be withstood, so at last the angel stepped aside from the doorway. When Tom looked through it, he saw that the garden had gone, and there was only a paved yard with dustbins, and in the middle stood old, old Mrs Bartholomew angrily saying: 'Who has been meddling with the Time of my grand-father clock?' Then Tom woke; and at once all the strange dream-things sank back again to the bottom of his mind and into it rushed the ideas and questions and incomplete pieces of reasoning from his waking hours.

Tom thought again: Time no longer—the angel on the grandfather clock had sworn it. But if Time is ever to end, that means that, here and now, Time itself is only a temporary thing. It can be dispensed with perhaps; or, rather, it can be dodged. Tom himself might be able to dodge behind Time's back and have the Past—that is, Hatty's Present and the garden—here, now and for ever. To manage that, of course, he must understand the work-ings of Time.

'What is Time?' Tom asked Aunt Gwen, when she brought him his early cup of tea; and his aunt, not believing she had heard him aright, replied that it was nearly seven o'clock.

'What is Time—I mean, how does Time *work*?' Tom asked his uncle at breakfast. According to him, how-ever, there was not one certain answer; people just had theories.

'Of course,' said Uncle Alan, 'it used to be thought . . .' and Tom listened attentively, and sometimes he seemed to understand, and then, sometimes he was sure he didn't. 'But modern theories of Time,' said Uncle Alan, 'the *most* modern theories . . .' and Tom began wondering if theories went in and out of fashion, like ladies' dresses, and then suddenly knew that he couldn't be attending, and wrenched his mind back, and thought again that he was understanding, and then again was sure he wasn't, and experienced a great depression.

'I've heard a theory, too,' said Tom, while his uncle paused to drink some tea. 'I know an angel—I know *of* an angel who said that, in the end, there would be Time no longer.'

'An angel!' His uncle's shout was so explosive that a great deal of tea slopped down his tie, and he was made even angrier to have to mop it up. 'What on earth have angels to do with scientific theories?' Tom trembled, and dared not explain that this was more than a theory: it was a blazing, angelic certitude.

Uncle Alan was saying, in an angry voice, that he didn't want any more breakfast. He went from the house, slamming the front door after him, and ten minutes early for work.

As soon as he had gone, Aunt Gwen said reproachfully to Tom: 'Tom, I wish you wouldn't.'

'Well,' said Tom, 'I didn't know he felt like that about angels, did I?'

'Your uncle is as reverent as anyone about angels, in their proper place,' said Aunt Gwen; 'but it's very bad for him to be crossed at breakfast-time. His nerves are always a little on edge so early in the morning, and before we know where we are he has lost his temper, and then he rushes over his breakfast or leaves half of it. It all leads to indigestion.'

'I'm sorry,' said Tom. Certainly his aunt had an insight

into Truth, although it was a different kind from his uncle's.

That evening, as soon as Alan Kitson came in, his wife took him aside to talk to him. At first he was inclined to talk too, and at a high pitch; but towards the end he was saying nothing; and at the very end there was a pause and then he said, 'Perhaps you are right: I ought to.'

At supper, when he saw Tom, he said, 'Tom, I apologize,' so majestically that Tom felt quite crushed beneath it.

Tom supposed that the subject of Time would be left to rest; but his uncle was now determined to make full amends for the morning. After supper he got out pencil and paper and began to draw diagrams for Tom. 'Imagine, Tom, that this is a point in Time . . .' Later he asked Tom to imagine a painter standing in a landscape and painting it, and a second painter coming behind him and painting the same landscape with the first painter's picture of the landscape in it, and yet a third painter coming up and painting the same landscape with the first painter's picture of the landscape and with the second painter's picture of the first painter's picture of the landscape, and then a fourth painter . . . 'I hope that parallel has made things clearer to you, Tom,' said his uncle. 'Or look at it another way. Suppose . . .' Tom's face was beginning to go stiff all over with the expression of understanding he was putting on it; and really, by now, he wanted just to cry, like a baby, because he understood nothing, and yet it was all so important to him.

Then, suddenly, Uncle Alan was mentioning Rip van

Winkle. 'For instance,' he said, 'think of Rip van Winkle —or no, perhaps that's not very illuminating. No, think, for instance, of a new point in Time which we'll call A.'

But Uncle Alan was too late: Tom had already begun thinking of Rip van Winkle, because he was the first person Uncle Alan had mentioned that Tom really knew anything about; indeed, Tom knew all about him. Rip van Winkle had gone out hunting one day in the North American mountains, and had fallen asleep in an enchanted place. It seemed to him that the time he spent sleeping there was only a night; but, when he woke up and went down the mountain-side to his family, he found that twenty years had gone by.

Now, thought Tom, wasn't he himself rather like Rip van Winkle in reverse, so to speak? Instead of going forward for twenty years, Tom went back a hundred and more, to Hatty's lifetime. He did not always go back to exactly the same Time, every night; nor did he take Time in its usual order. The fir-tree, for instance: he had seen it standing, fallen and then standing again—it was still standing last night. He had seen Hatty as a girl of his own age, then as a much younger one, and recently as a girl who —although Tom would not yet fully admit it—was outgrowing him altogether. In flashes, Tom had seen Hatty's Time—the garden's Time—covering what must be about ten years, while his own Time achieved only the weeks of a summer holiday.

'You might say,' Tom said slowly, coming into the conversation again without having been listening to it,

M

'You might say that different people have different times, although of course, they're really all bits of the same big Time.'

'Well,' said his uncle, 'one could say more accurately ——'

Tom went straight on. 'So that I might be able, for some reason, to step back into someone else's Time, in the Past; or, if you like'—he saw it all, suddenly and for the first time, from Hatty's point of view—'she might step forward into my Time, which would seem the Future to her, although to me it seems the Present.'

'It would be much clearer, Tom,' said his uncle, 'to go back to this Point A——'

But Tom was going on. 'Whichever way it is, she would be no more a ghost from the Past than I would be a ghost from the Future. We're neither of us ghosts; and the garden isn't either. That settles that.'

'What are you talking about?' Uncle Alan said irritably. 'Gardens? And what settles what? We're talking of possibilities—theories.'

'But,' said Tom, 'suppose someone really had stepped out of one Time into another—just like that—then that would be proof.'

'*Proof!*' cried Uncle Alan; and for a moment Tom thought he was going to be angry again, but he controlled himself. 'I have been able to explain to you very little, Tom, if I have not even conveyed to you that proof— in matters of Time Theory—*Proof. . .* !' Apparently, about Time, as about some master-criminal, you could prove nothing.

Tom did not mind. He had settled some things to his own satisfaction. Starting from what the angel had revealed to him, he had worked out something useful about the nature of Time. At least, he did not quite see yet how it would be useful, but he had a warm, excited feeling in his mind that seemed to him to mean that he was on the verge of finding—round and perfect—the solution of his problem.

That Wednesday night Tom went down to the garden in a new frame of mind. The season was still winter; but Tom looked round about him sharply, thinking, 'I daresay, but is this the *same* winter? Is this a different bit of Hatty's Time that I have come into? If so, is it an earlier bit or a later bit?'

This question was answered for him when, walking round the garden, he came to the hedge: a gateway had been made in it, to lead into the meadow. The thing had certainly not been there on Tom's last visit, or he would have noticed it at once. The gate had been put in since then, and had had time to grow old-looking and shabby.

The gravel-path under Tom's feet was crackly with frost as he went towards the gate; and when he leaned over it and looked across what in summer he had known as low-lying grazing ground, he saw one expanse of ice. On the far side of the meadow, where the ice was best, skaters were moving, skimming the surface, calling to each other, laughing.

Tom felt left out of the fun. He was sure that this was one of the parties of friends into which James had said he would draw Hatty. One could guess which among the skating-party might be Hatty herself: a girl who was among all the others at one moment, and then, at the next, would be speeding alone over the ice. A habit of solitude in early childhood is not easily broken. Indeed, it may prove lifelong.

Now the young men among the skaters were pulling curved branches off the pollarded willow-trees, to make sticks for a practice game of bandy, or ice-hockey; a stone was to be the ball. The girls gathered to watch, laughing and talking.

The solitary skater had swerved away from them, and now came rushing across the ice on her skates—right across the meadow towards the hedge. Hatty—for it *was* Hatty—had seen Tom. 'Or at least, I saw something and I thought it might be you.' She peered doubtfully at Tom, even as she was gliding up on her last, long stroke.

She was opening the garden gate. 'I'm so glad it *is* you, Tom! I miss you sometimes, even now—in spite of the Chapman girls being good fun, and Barty and the others—in spite of the skating—Oh, Tom, skating! I feel as if I could go from here to the end of the world, if all the world were ice! I feel as free as a bird—as I've never felt before! I want to go so far—so far!'

She was urging him on to the ice now, nor was Tom unwilling. 'Come on, Tom, do!' He felt the smoothness of the ice beneath his one bare foot, and the very slightest spring and sway of it, like a ballroom floor, under Hatty's weight. As though the ice made an enchantment, he forgot the problem of Time he had to think of—forgot that he had anything to think of. Hatty swooped away from him, and he swooped after her on a more glorious ice-slide than he and Peter had ever found in the streets at home; but his sliding ended sooner than Hatty's skating, and his action was earthbound, whilst hers was like a strong bird's.

'Tom,' Hatty called softly to him, from over the ice, but speeding nearer, passing him with a rush of air, 'why haven't you skates?'

'Oh, why haven't I skates?' Tom repeated in anguish, for all the skates he had ever used had been hired ones on a town ice-rink; and his uncle and aunt would not have skates, he was sure; and they would think it very odd if he wanted to buy skates in a great hurry in the middle of summer.

Then, like a brilliant, icy light, came an idea into Tom's head—one of the most daring ideas he had ever had.

With outspread arms he begged Hatty to stop skating and listen to him; and she did. 'Hatty, where do you keep your skates, when you're not using them, I mean?'

'In the boot cupboard in the hall. At the end of the winter, I oil the straps and grease the blades and wrap the skates up in paper, and they go on to the top shelf of the cupboard.'

There were no skates in the hall-cupboard in the day-time, Tom knew—nothing on the shelves but the things that the ginger-bearded tenant used for the care of his car. If Hatty had kept her skates there, then, of course, when the Melbournes had all died or moved house, long ago, her skates would have been turned out of the cupboard, perhaps to be sold, or given or thrown away. Anyway, they would have been lost to him.

Before Hatty had finished explaining about the boot cupboard, Tom had decided that it was quite the wrong place for her to keep her skates: she needed somewhere dry and safe, of course, but above all somewhere secret.

'Hatty, will you promise me something?'

'What?'

'Will you promise first?'

'I can't promise anything that's wrong or dangerous.'

'It isn't either. I only want you to promise first, because otherwise, when you hear what it is, you might just say it was too silly—and it isn't—really it isn't.'

'Well, tell me, and then I'll promise if I possibly can.'

Tom had to be satisfied with this, so he said, 'Well, I only want you to keep your skates, always, when you're not using them, in that secret place you showed me in your bedroom cupboard, under the floorboards.'

'*There!*' said Hatty, as though it were a very long time since she had needed to think of that place. 'But that *is* silly—why ever should I keep them there?'

'Promise!' cried Tom. 'It only seems silly; but there's no harm in it. Promise. It's nothing to you.'

'What is it to you?' Hatty asked, bewildered.

'It's too long to tell you now; but promise—promise on your honour—always to keep your skates there, when you're not skating—in that secret place. It still is secret, isn't it?' he added with sudden fear.

'The only person I ever told was you,' said Hatty. 'But, Tom——'

'Promise on your honour, as you said you would if you could,' Tom insisted, and saw that he was winning.

'I don't understand, but—all right, I promise—I promise on my honour.'

Tom had perfect faith in her; he turned at once and slid back to the gate, towards the house.

'But, here!' Hatty cried after him, as an idea occurred to her. 'Come back, Tom! That promise means I should have to leave the skates behind altogether if I went away from here.'

That was quite true, but Tom did not stop. He heard Hatty's cry as he went; and he also heard the more distant shouts of the skaters calling to her, asking what she was doing all by herself by the garden gate, calling her to rejoin their sport.

He ran into the house and upstairs. He took away the bedroom slipper wedging the front door of the flat, and shut the door; but, all the same, he intended going out and down into the garden again that very night. With luck, he needed only five minutes in the flat, and then he would be down again in the meadow with Hatty, skating.

He needed no light in his bedroom. He felt for the cupboard door and opened it, and then felt among the cracks of the floorboards inside. He had to fetch his penknife from his trouser pocket before he could lever the right one up. He felt in the space underneath and touched two largish objects wrapped in paper.

His hands were at the paper wrappings when he heard a door open—the door of the other bedroom in the flat. He realized that, in his excitement, he must have been making more noise than he should have done. They had heard him; they were coming.

He closed the cupboard door as tar as he could, without clicking it, and slid swiftly into bed. He was only just in time; a second later his aunt opened his bedroom door and switched on the light. He covered his creaking of the bed-springs, which she must have heard, by turning noisily in bed, with his eyes still shut, and moaning, as if in a bad dream. His aunt came over to him, felt his forehead to make sure he had no fever, kissed him and went out again. She left his bedroom door ajar behind her; Tom heard her go into her own room, but he did not hear her close the door of that either. She had left them both open in order to be able to listen for him.

Tom lay wide-eyed in bed, quivering with impatience, knowing that the slightest sound might bring his aunt back. He would have to wait until she was asleep again, and how long that might be he could not know.

In the end, it was Tom who slept first—slept and dreamt of skating to the world's end and the end of Time.

XXII

The Forgotten Promise

WHEN Tom woke, on Thursday morning, his first thought was that he had missed his precious chance of going back to the garden last night; his second thought was for the hiding-place under the floorboards.

Almost he thought that he must have dreamt of the discovery, but when he opened the cupboard door there was the raised floorboard with his penknife beside it. He saw the two brown-paper packages in the hole, drew them out and unwrapped them: they were a pair of skates, with boots still screwed and strapped to them.

Then he saw a slip of paper left behind in the floor-cavity. He brought it out and read what was written on it:

'*To whomever may find this.* These skates are the property of *Harriet Melbourne* but she leaves them in this place in fulfilment of a promise she once made to a little boy.'

The note was signed, and dated June 20. The year was there too, but so smudged by the death of some insect that Tom could only read the first two numbers: a one and an eight.

Tom spent a good deal of that day gloating over Hatty's skates—his skates. They were of an older fashion than Tom knew, and belonged to an older fashion of skating, too. They were Fen Runners, whose blades end in a long, curved prow to cut through the rougher surfaces of outdoor ice, as the skater travels mile after mile over the great frozen distances that the Fens afford.

He tended the skates as best he could. He said nothing to his uncle or aunt; but he looked for emery paper, and at last found some in his uncle's tool box, and rubbed the rust off the skate-blades. The blades ought to have been re-ground, perhaps, but that was more than Tom could manage. He borrowed a bottle of olive oil from his aunt's larder, and oiled the wooden foot-stock and the parched leather of the straps and the boots. He tried on the boots: they were almost a perfect fit—perhaps a little on the large size, but that was all to the good. He could wear two pairs of socks inside them.

While Tom was oiling the boots, the thing he had so long been seeking for came to him: the solution—rounded and perfect—of his problem of Time.

His aunt was out shopping, so that Tom was working with the olive oil quite openly on the kitchen-table. The kitchen clock was facing him—staring at him intently; and suddenly Tom thought of that night—many nights ago now—when he had returned its gaze, at first with disbelief, and then with an immense wonder. The clock had told him then that, whereas he took several minutes to get downstairs to the garden door and then up again, he took no time at all to wander all round the garden. However long a time he spent in the garden, the kitchen clock measured none of it. He spent time there, without spending a fraction of a second of ordinary time. That was perhaps what the grandfather clock had meant by striking a thirteenth hour: the hours after the twelfth do not exist in ordinary Time; they are not bound by the laws of ordinary Time; they are not over in sixty ordinary minutes; they are endless.

Tom rubbed the oil along the straps, and his reasoning seemed smooth and right: he could spend an endless time in the garden, if he liked. He could, after all, have both things—the garden and his family—because he could stay for ever in the garden, and yet for ever his family would be expecting him next Saturday afternoon. Time here would stand still at Thursday, and wait for him; it would only start again if he left the garden and came back to the flat.

'I could stay in the garden for ever,' Tom told the kitchen clock, and laughed for joy; and then shivered a little, because 'for ever' sounded long and lonely. 'But, anyway,' he reasoned, 'tonight I could try it out: I could stay just a few days or a few weeks or a year perhaps; but if I get tired of it'—he really meant, if he grew homesick— 'well, then, I can always come back. And then there is another chance on Friday night: I can stay longer then— only come back after I've seen everything in the garden, and done everything.'

Tom thought of all the delights of the garden while he tended his skates. By the time the work was done, he was settled in his mind, and happy. He was ready for the night.

Only one thing went badly amiss that Thursday. Just as he was getting into bed, he remembered: 'I never wrote to Peter yesterday!'

'Never mind,' said his aunt, tucking him up.

'But I promised to.'

'It's bad to break a promise, but I'm sure you didn't mean to. Luckily, it won't matter very much to Peter. Why, he'll be seeing you the day after tomorrow.'

Tom knew that it did matter. The broken promise was bad enough; but he knew, as well, that Peter would be feeling desperate without his letter. Peter needed all that Tom could write to him, to feed his imaginings—to feed his dreams. 'Write to me more about the garden and Hatty,' he had begged Tom. 'Tell me what you did . . . Be sure to tell me what you're going to do.'

'Sorry, Pete,' Tom murmured into his pillow, and felt wretched. He hoped that Peter had by now got over the bitterness of this betrayal. Peter went to bed earlier than Tom, so that probably he had already ended his day of disappointment with sleep.

In this, Tom was wrong: Peter was still awake, grieving. He had had no letter from Tom today, and he did not know why—Tom did not lightly forget promises. He did not know what Tom had been doing last night and the night before; he did not know what secrets Tom might now be master of; he did not know what wonderful things Tom might be doing this very night.

Peter stared and stared across the half-darkness of his bedroom, until his eyes blurred with tears and then cleared again. He longed, more than ever he had done before, to be with Tom—to know what he was doing. He fell asleep at last with that longing in his mind; and the last view that his eyes closed upon was Tom's postcard view of Ely, on the bedroom mantelpiece opposite.

Tom fell asleep too; but woke promptly when the time came. He put on his two pairs of socks. This time he left both of his bedroom slippers to wedge open the front door of the flat; carrying the skates, he went downstairs. Of course, it was quite possible that the season outside was no longer winter, after all—and yet he felt sure that it was. When he opened the door, he found that he was right. A deep frost lay everywhere, binding fast the trees and all the plants of the garden so that there seemed not the slightest movement or life. The garden might have been sculptured in stone. Such a frost there was.

In the deep silence, Tom heard his name whispered hesitantly from behind him. He turned. Hatty was standing in the hall, dressed in thick, warm clothes, with a fur cap on her head and with a fur muff, in which her hands were concealed.

'I wasn't sure if it were you, Tom, or a trick of the frost-light.'

'Of course it's me,' said Tom, and really wondered whether Hatty's eyesight were failing.

'I was hoping you might turn up—you and no one else. Look!' Hatty withdrew one hand from her muff, and Tom saw that, tucked inside it, was her pair of skates. In reply, he held up his own. Hatty nodded in satisfaction; but she did not seem struck by any similarity of appearance. She did not know what Tom knew.

'James will be down in a minute,' said Hatty. 'It's his turn to go to market in Castleford, and I'm going with him. He doesn't know that I mean to skate this afternoon, and where to. I mean to skate right down to Ely.'

'Can you?' asked Tom, awed.

Hatty misunderstood him. 'Well, of course, I shouldn't. It really isn't quite ladylike, so I mustn't tell anyone of it; and yet it would be even more improper to go alone ...'

'But I meant, is the river really frozen over?'

'Frozen so hard, Tom—why, Abel's grandfather says this is one of the hardest, longest frosts he's ever known. The river's frozen from above here to below Castleford and below Ely. The river here is too near the source for the ice to be safe, but below Castleford and all through the Fens—Oh, Tom, do come with me!'

Tom was excited, and yet aghast. 'Now? Without going into the garden at all? Without even going through it?'

'The garden will always be there,' Hatty coaxed him; 'but this great frost——'

She stopped speaking suddenly and turned to face the stairs, down which someone was now coming. Tom made up his mind quickly, and advanced to stand beside Hatty: he would leave the garden for the time being, and go with her.

The newcomer was James, and he, too, was dressed for going out. He greeted Hatty, and took his market bag and two thick travelling rugs off one of the hall brackets. Then all three of them went out by the front door—the front door of the Melbournes' house, through which Tom had never before gone.

Outside in the drive, a pony and trap were waiting, with Abel at the pony's head. Abel's expression, at the sight of Tom, clearly said, 'Never thought to see *you* again!' All the old horror had vanished from his look.

They climbed into the trap, and the rugs were wrapped round James and Hatty. Abel took the opportunity to give Tom a private, friendly wink. Then James flopped the reins along the pony's back, and they started off: down the Melbournes' drive, up a lane with an orchard on one side and a meadow on the other, turn right at a white-washed cottage, then five miles or more of a brisk, ringing trot on ice-bound roads between ice-bound fields and meadows. To the east of them lay the low hills that look like sleeping giants in that flat countryside; to the west of them, unseen, wound the river, taking the same direction as the high road, towards Castleford.

Tom had been this way before with his uncle and aunt, but the view then had always been shut out by houses; and he had always gone by bus or car. Indeed, never in all his .

life had he travelled behind a horse. Now he watched in fascination the muscular movement of the pony's fore-shortened back and its hindquarters, almost under his feet; he felt the harsh springiness on the untyred wheels as they bowled along.

They reached Castleford in a market-day throng. James put up the pony and trap at the University Arms (an odd name for the inn, since Castleford has no University); many of the farmers, millers and other businessmen from the country parts seemed to be doing the same. Then James, market-bag in hand, prepared to go his way. 'Do you want a lift back later, Hatty?'

'Thank you, Cousin James,' she said; 'but I don't quite know when I shall be ready to return.'

'There's always the train,' he said; and so they parted.

In the streets of Castleford many people were carrying skates. Some were making for the river where it passes beneath the bridges of Castleford, between sloping lawns of grass. The ice here was already good; but the distances to be skated could not be great. Hatty was after something better. She took some of the narrower back-streets, darted—with Tom after her—down a certain Gas Lane, and so brought him at last to the river where it begins to leave Castleford, broadening and deepening as it goes. Here it prepares to enter the Fenland, where many other waterways—lodes and cuts and drains, with a man-made directness, rivers with ancient meanderings—will, in their own time, join it. The stream that flowed narrowly, across the meadow from Hatty's garden, becomes already, before Ely, the Great Ouse; below Ely, the greatness

of the Ouse swallows up whole rivers, like the Lark
and the Wissey; and so it goes on, to be swallowed up
itself in the greatness of the sea. All these and other
Fenland waters, at the time of Tom's visit, were in the
grip of a memorable frost.

XXIII

Skating

THAT winter the frost had begun at the end of December and went on—with a milder spell for a week in January—to the beginning of March. It was of the greatest severity. Even running waters froze at last. Ice stopped the wheels of the upriver water-mills, and blocked the way for the barges that, in those days, plied from King's Lynn as far upstream as the hithes of Castleford.

The frost was over all England. On some waters oxen were roasted whole, as though that proved what a fine frost this was, and what ice was best used for. On the Cherwell, at Oxford, a coach with six horses was driven down the middle of the frozen river, to the great satisfaction of all concerned. But the people of Castleford and the Fens knew the truest and greatest and best use of ice: they skated.

There had been skating on the river for several weeks when Tom and Hatty came down to it; and it seemed to them as if there must be more people skating than could possibly be doing market-day business in the town.

Not everyone skated well or fast: there were some learners, and a policeman who moved with the dignified pace of a navy-blue swan. There was also the newer fashion of skating—figure-skating: Hatty pointed it out to Tom. In one place an orange had been set centrally upon the ice, and four top-hatted, dignified gentlemen were describing a harmony of figures to it—from it—round it. Suddenly a town-urchin, on rusty Fen runners, partly strapped, partly tied with string to his boots, dashed in, snatched up the orange and dashed away again with his teeth already in it. The swaying, shifting crowd of skaters closed up behind him, and the figure-skating gentlemen stopped skating, and were extremely annoyed.

Like Tom, Hatty laughed aloud at the impudence of the theft; but all the time she was looking round her sharply and a little nervously. Among all the townspeople and countrypeople, someone might recognize her, and pass comment on her being there alone. However, Hatty was fortunate: no one seemed to notice her at all.

The skates were on, and now Hatty and Tom were ready

for the ice: two skaters on one pair of skates, which seemed to Tom both the eeriest and the most natural thing in the world. A new skill and power came into him, as though these skates knew their work better than the skater: he could skate as well as Hatty, because he had her skates. The only difference between them was that his blades left no cut or bruise upon the surface of the ice in travelling over it.

They did not skate with linked hands, as many skating partners did, for fear of the odd appearance being noticed; but, once they had left behind the thick crowds of sociable skaters just below the town, they skated abreast, keeping time together, stroke for stroke. There was no wind at all that afternoon, and they cut through the still air faster and faster.

Hatty had pinned her skirt up above her ankles, for greater freedom of movement; and now she abandoned the use of her muff, the better to swing her arms in time with their skating. Their speed made the muff fly out behind her, on its cord, and at last a stroke gave it such a violent fling that the cord broke and the fur ball of the muff shot away and landed in the middle of a game of bandy and somehow became part of the game, and was never seen again. Hatty saw it disappear, and neither stopped nor faltered in her course, but only laughed, as though she cared nothing now for muffs or improprieties or aunts. They skated on.

They left the Castleford reaches altogether. They came to a lock, with its gates frozen fast, and its weir frozen too: they hobbled ashore and round the lock and on to the ice again. They skated under a bridge, and, even in the shelter of it, the ice bore strongly. All the ferryways were frozen as they went, with the ferrymen standing sourly by their ice-locked boats.

Hatty and Tom skated on and on. The skaters they met now were mostly men. There were few girls, that Tom could see, and none without escort. They came to a lonely river-side alehouse: its signboard said: 'The Five Miles from Anywhere—No Hurry.' Here there were skaters, labourers from the Fen farms, resting on the bank. They called out jovially to Hatty, asking if she would like any of them to skate with her for company. They went on calling, until she called back that she had a companion with her, even if they could not see him. The skaters thought this a good hoax and laughed, taking no offence; and Hatty laughed; and Tom laughed too, but no one except Hatty heard him.

They skated on, and the thin, brilliant sun was beginning to set, and Hatty's black shadow flitted along at their right hand, across the dazzle of the ice. Sometimes they skated on the main river; sometimes they skated along the flooded washes. Only the willows along the bank watched them; and the ice hissed with their passage.

They had stopped talking or thinking—their legs and arms and bodies seemed to throw from side to side with the precise, untiring regularity of clock-pendulums—long before Hatty cried: 'Look, Tom—the tower of Ely cathedral!'

From the river, however, Ely's tower plays a game with the traveller. Hatty and Tom skated and skated, and for a long time the tower seemed to let them come no nearer, but performed a mysterious movement instead, now to one side, now to the other, now ahead, according to the windings of the river. At last, however, they were certainly getting nearer, and now the cathedral tower began to disappear behind the nearer rooftops; and here they were where the river curves in to the town of Ely.

They went ashore. Hatty unstrapped and unscrewed her skates and walked in her skating-boots—she had no others; Tom slung his boots and skates round his neck and walked in his socks.

They walked through the town, making for the cathedral, and went in through the great west door. Inside, the failing of winter daylight was beginning to fill the vastness with gloom. Through this they walked down the nave towards the octagon; and it seemed to Tom as if the roof of the cathedral were like a lesser sky, for, although they walked steadily, when they looked upwards, they had moved very little in relation to its spaces. Hatty walked with dazzled eyes: 'Oh, I never thought there was anywhere so big—so beautiful!' she said.

They passed a verger, and Tom whispered to Hatty: 'Ask about going up the tower.' She turned back and did so. The verger said the young lady could go up if she would be waiting by the font at the west end, in ten minutes from now. It was the last ascent of the day. The charge was sixpence.

They spent the interval in walking round the cathedral. As they came out of the Lady Chapel, Tom lingered to read a memorial tablet to a certain Mr Robinson, Gentleman of the City, who had exchanged Time for Eternity on the 15th day of October one thousand eight hundred and twelve at the age of seventy-two. Tom reflected that, in a way, he was intending to copy Mr Robinson; he meant to exchange ordinary Time, that would otherwise move on towards Saturday, for an endless Time—an Eternity—in the garden. 'Exchanged Time for Eternity,' Tom repeated aloud, and noticed that the walls of the cathedral returned not the slightest echo of his voice. The silence was chilling.

Hatty had turned back to see what kept Tom. Now, over his shoulder, she too read the inscription, and her attention was caught by the same quaint phrase: 'Exchanged Time for Eternity,' she read aloud. 'Time . . . Eternity . . .' the words spoken by Hatty made a little echo, and her voice and its echo filled the silence after Tom's speaking, so that he was somehow comforted by the sound. Impulsively he turned to Hatty: he would confide in her —he would tell her all that he intended. He would do it now.

But Hatty was looking towards the font: already people were waiting there, and she moved to join them. Nor did Tom wish to delay her, for he, too, wanted to go up the tower. He followed Hatty. After all, he could talk to her later, when they had started the long run home to Castleford. He would have plenty of time then.

XXIV

Brothers Meet

P ETER LONG slept only a little that Thursday night before he woke himself in dissatisfaction: his dreaming was all wrong. Night after night he had managed to dream that he was with Tom; he had been able to dream of the garden, as Tom described it in his letters. Tonight, when his ignorance of Tom's plans made him yearn all the more to imagine what he might be doing—tonight, he could not dream of the garden at all. Instead, he had begun dreaming of a tall grey shape that rode like an anchored ship in the surrounding level. He did not know what he was seeing, until his eyes opened from sleep and fell at once upon the Ely postcard, still dimly visible on the mantelpiece by the light from the street.

Peter closed his eyes again, to shut out the sight of the cathedral tower. He concentrated his thoughts upon what Tom might be doing at this very moment; and, at the same time, he began to count, in order to send himself off to sleep. He did not count the usual sheep going through a stile, because there are neither sheep nor stiles in a garden: he simply counted.

Numbers, in their regularity, began to send Peter to sleep. He had a drowsy feeling that he was earnestly seeking for Tom, and that pleased him; surely he would see the garden soon. He had only to follow Tom . . . He was really asleep now; but even in his sleep he went on counting, and the numbers now began to be numbers of something particular. The garden was still not reached; and these were numbers of steps that he was counting—steps upward, winding inside a grey tower that, even in his dream, he perceived with annoyance to be the cathedral tower of Ely once again.

There are nearly three hundred steps up to the top of the tower of Ely cathedral, or—to be exact—two hundred and eighty-six. At least, that is what Tom made them, counting as he climbed. He was at the end of the file of sightseers; Hatty just before him.

They came stooping out at last through a little door on to the leads of the tower roof. Now, nothing was higher. They looked over the parapet and saw the roof of the great nave below them. They looked far down over the house-tops of Ely, and saw the black holes of the chimney-pots, through which mounted the smoke of winter fires. The lines of smoke were beginning to bend slightly out of the upright as a little wind got up. The breath of this wind and the puffing of a train in Ely station was all the sound that reached them.

They saw the town and, at once, beyond it, for Ely is very small. They saw the river bounding the town on one side; and they looked along it, downstream. They saw the whiteness of that iceway, gleaming where the sunset touched it, and winding and disappearing into distant mist and evening, in the direction of Littleport, Denver, King's Lynn and the sea. Then they looked back along the way they had come, from Castleford: they were awed at the distance of it.

The tower-keeper pointed to something far away that he declared were the spires of Castleford; then he drew his sightseeing party aside to peer in another direction, to-wards Peterborough. Hatty went with the others.

Tom remained where he was, still staring towards Castleford. He was alone on that side of the leads for a moment; and then he had a strong feeling that he was not alone after all. Someone had come belatedly out through the door from the spiral staircase, and now stood beside him. He knew, even before he turned, that it was Peter.

From the other side of the leads, Hatty looked round to see where Tom had got to. She saw, instead of one boy, two: they were very much alike, and dressed identically in pyjamas. The second boy had the same insubstantial look that she had noticed recently in Tom himself: she was almost sure that she could see the tower parapet through them both. She stared in wonderment.

'But, Tom, where's the garden?' Peter was saying, rather querulously. 'I thought you were with Hatty, in the garden.'

Tom answered directly, because he felt in his bones that time was short, and shortening. 'The garden's back there,' he said briefly, flinging his arm outwards, in the direction of Castleford. 'And Hatty's here.'

'Where? I can't see her,' said Peter.

Tom was pointing with his finger, and Peter was facing Hatty across the leads—she was the only one among the sightseers who had turned in his direction.

'There!' said Tom. 'Right opposite to you—the one carrying skates.'

'But that'—said Peter indignantly—'that's not Hatty: that's a grown-up woman!'

Tom, staring at Hatty as though he were seeing her for the first time, opened his mouth to speak; but he could not.

'Time'—called the tower-keeper—'time to go down again, if you please, ladies and gentlemen!'

The little crowd of sightseers began to cluster round the doorway to the spiral staircase; one by one they began to go through it. Only Hatty remained where she was, and the two boys.

'But she's grown-up,' Peter said again.

Hatty began to come across to them; and Tom felt Peter shrinking away from her.

'Who was he? What was he?' Hatty breathed to Tom; and Tom, again without looking, knew that Peter had vanished from his side—thinned out and vanished. 'He was like you,' Hatty whispered; 'and he was unreal-looking, just like you.'

'Come along, lady!' called the tower-keeper, and looked at Hatty curiously, thinking she was young to be queer in the head and muttering to herself.

'He was my brother, Peter,' Tom stammered; 'but he's real, Hatty. He's real, like me. You agreed I was real, Hatty.'

'Don't you want to get home at all tonight, young miss?' the keeper was asking impatiently.

Hatty heard him, and looked up and round her suddenly: the sun had set; in the town, yellow lights were springing up in the windows; beyond the town, the Fen level was one shadowy expanse, so that one could no longer see the windings of the river.

'It's late,' she cried, in fright. 'Yes, we must hurry!'

'*We?*' said the keeper. 'It's you should hurry! Here I've been waiting for you——' Hatty, however, now started down the stairway, in great haste, with Tom at her heels; and the keeper was left to grumble to himself and lock up and come after them.

Inside the tower, it was as black as if night had already

descended: Tom felt that the darkness increased Hatty's anxiety for the homeward journey. The hurry, and the fear behind it, prevented Tom from thinking coolly about the strange meeting above, and about what had been said then. He wondered confusedly how Peter had come to them, and whether he would come again.

That did not happen. Peter Long, at home had woken up from his dream—a bad dream, if not quite a nightmare. He lay in bed remembering it, but only in seemingly un-connected parts: he had been counting to send himself to sleep, and he remembered getting as far as two hundred and eighty-six; then, he had been at some great height, where he did not want to be, and the garden was impossibly far away; Tom had been there, too, somehow; and he remem-bered Tom's pointing someone out to him and saying that she was Hatty, and his own crying out that it could not be so, because this was a grown-up young woman and not a child at all. He remembered then the look on Tom's face: a strange, dawning amazement, and fear.

Tom and Hatty hurried from the cathedral and went down to the river again, just when most of the Ely skaters were beginning to come off it. They were the only two, it seemed, who were starting to skate.

Three old men, past skating themselves, were leaning on convenient posts along the waterfront, watching all that was going on. They considered themselves of the age and experience to give Hatty advice. One asked where she was skating to, at that time of evening; and when she said, 'Castleford,' they all three shook their heads.

'If the ice holds,' said one; 'but this old south-west wind

means rain and thaw, likely.' The breeze that Tom and Hatty had noticed from the top of the tower had by now strengthened into a real wind; it felt softer and milder, even in Tom's face, than the former frosty stillness.

'There's already someone went through, I heard,' said the second old man. 'Somewhere upstream it was. He didn't drown, though. There were friends with him, and they got him out just in time, with a ladder over the ice. There'll be a hole left, and rotten ice round it: you'd best keep a look-out for it. Now, where did they say it was, Matthew?'

The first old man did not know; but the third one thought the hole must be a biggish one, and that Hatty would be sure to notice it when she got really close to it. She must not forget to be careful, too, of treacherous ice under bridges and trees, and along reed-beds.

The first old man started the round again by saying that Hatty would do better to go by train from Ely to Castleford.

Hatty thanked them all, but went on fastening her skate straps: Tom thought she was rather brave. They stood up together on the ice, and Hatty wished the old men a cheerful good night; and they earnestly wished her the best of luck, and one of them shouted after her that at least she would have a full moon. When they had skated out of earshot, Hatty told Tom that she had not had enough money to take the train all the way from Ely to Castleford.

They were skating out against a stream of homecomers, but soon they passed the last of them and were skating alone. Tom knew that this was the time to talk to Hatty, and yet, clearly, she was disinclined for any conversation: all her powers were being put forth into her skating. Tom stole sideways glances at her as she went, weighing in his mind what Peter had said; he did not speak to her.

The moon rose, full, as the old men had said: it had a halo to it, which is supposed to mean rain. The moonlight laid open their way before them, and yet made it appear more desolate, and themselves more lonely. Except for the wind and the sound of steel on ice, there was silence. Neither Hatty nor Tom liked the silence; but neither broke it. In silence, moonlight and loneliness they were gliding onwards.

Some way ahead, on the river-bank to their right, they noticed an upright, dark shape, perhaps six feet high. It was certainly a post or a tree-trunk; and they were paying no particular attention to it. Then, suddenly, they saw it move.

Hatty gave a little gasp, but never stopped skating—it was almost as if she could not. At this curve of the river she was skating full into the moonlight, but the man—for it was a man—was black against it, and seemed unnaturally tall. He seemed to be watching something intently, and Tom felt that he was watching them.

They were nearer now; they would be level soon. The figure on the bank stirred again, and called over the ice a name that was between a question and a hail: 'Miss Hatty . . .'

Tom felt himself fall out of stroke with Hatty, as she wavered in her course.

'Who is it?' she called; but Tom thought she recognized

the voice, although he did not. Her strokes were beginning to shorten; her course was curving towards the bank.

'It's me, young Barty.'

'Oh, Barty, I am glad to see you!' cried Hatty, forgetting shyness in her relief.

He came down to the edge of the bank—a well-set young man in a caped overcoat, wearing farmer's gaiters. 'But where are you off to, all alone, at this time of evening, on this ice?'

'To Castleford. From there I can take the train, or walk home. I must get home.'

'As to getting home—why, yes,' agreed young Barty; 'but you shouldn't be skating alone like this. I'd best give you a lift.'

It seemed that he had been on his way home from Castleford market, in his gig. He had turned aside down a drove-way to have a look at the river and the condition of the ice. That was when Tom and Hatty had seen him.

Delightfully, the horse and gig, although invisible from the river, were only a few yards away, on the other side of the river embankment. When young Barty had helped Hatty up this embankment they saw the horse waiting between the shafts, lit by the little yellow flames of the head-lamps—the first warm-coloured light they had seen since the candlelight and lamplight in the house windows of Ely. Beyond the gig, the drove-way stretched back to meet the main road to Castleford and home.

They all got into the gig, young Barty and Hatty at either end of the front seat, with a large space in the middle which Tom took for himself.

'I'll drive you to Waterbeach,' said young Barty. 'You can take a train from there to Castleford. If you'll excuse the question—have you enough money for the ticket? If not, I could lend you some.'

'That is very kind,' said Hatty, primly. Then she added, 'I fear that I take you out of your way.'

She certainly was not taking him on the way he had been going, which was home to one of his father's farms out in the Fens. Yet, without exactly telling an untruth, young Barty gave Hatty to understand that all this was a pleasure.

After that they drove in silence.

When they reached Waterbeach they found that the last train to Castleford had gone.

'I'll drive you to Castleford, then,' said young Barty, and sounded quite cheerful about it. So they went on again, and Tom noticed that this time the other two made more conversation. They remarked upon the weather and their journey, Hatty speaking at first awkwardly, and then with more ease. Young Barty said he had talked with James that afternoon on Castleford market; and now Tom remembered hearing of this young man as one of the friends of the Melbourne cousins. They had all been at school together in Castleford.

Soon, very naturally, Hatty and young Barty were talking of skating. Young Barty admired Hatty's achievement that day. He had done as much himself, certainly, this very winter; but few ladies had skated so far. His own mother had done so—he remembered the tale of it. Years ago, when old Barty and she had been courting, there had been one of these same widespread, hard frosts. The two of

o

them had gone skating together from Castleford to Ely and then to Littleport and beyond. They had skated so far and so long that the young woman had nearly fallen asleep as she skated, and she had half-dreamed that she and her sweetheart had reached the sea and were skating over the smoothed-out, frozen waves of it, to far countries.

He and Hatty laughed over that. Then young Barty began to speak of the prospects of further skating that winter, and of next winter. He loved skating, as Hatty did.

Tom found the conversation uninteresting, chiefly because he could not join in it. He was also cross with Hatty: she was behaving as if she either did not remember him or did not see him—or both. Several times a gesture of her hand actually passed through him. Once she leant her arm along the back of the gig-seat, as she turned the better to listen to young Barty, and then her wrist and hand rested in Tom's gullet and made his swallowing feel strange.

He was glad when they reached Castleford railway station. The last train had not gone, but there was a long time to wait for it: young Barty said it would be much better to drive home the last five miles, and Hatty did not object. Tom did, but he could not argue. He had been hoping for an empty railway compartment for that long, private, explanatory talk with Hatty: he *must* have it soon.

The gig drove on. Tom sat alone in his thoughts, while the other two talked over him or through him, with an increasing delight in each other's company. A village church clock struck across the darkened countryside, and Tom thought of Time: how he had been sure of mastering it, and of exchanging his own Time for an Eternity of Hatty's and so of living pleasurably in the garden for ever. The garden was still there, but meanwhile Hatty's Time had stolen a march on him, and had turned Hatty herself from his playmate into a grown-up woman. What Peter had seen was true.

Through the clattering of the horse's hooves, Tom listened to Hatty and young Barty: theirs was grown-up conversation, and had no interest for him; and his own thoughts displeased him. Gradually his mind fell into vacancy. He was not tired by the skating, nor was he sleepy because of the lateness of the hour, yet he slept: perhaps the monotony of the hoofbeats had something to do with it; perhaps a strange feeling that he was not in Hatty's thoughts any longer made him feel less awake and alive.

Dimly he felt the swing of the gig as it turned the corner by the whitewashed cottage and started down the lane to the big house.

When Mrs Melbourne, coldly amazed and angry, came to the front door to receive them, she saw only two people in the gig: that was to be expected. But even Hatty saw only one other besides herself, and that was young Barty.

XXV

Last Chance

O N Friday morning, in the peaceful hour before the others were awake, Aunt Gwen leaned out of bed, boiled the electric kettle and made an early pot of tea. She poured out a cup for her husband, one for herself, and then she rose to take the third to Tom.

She was crossing the little hall with the tea, when she

stopped dead, frozen at what she saw: the front door of the flat, which Alan himself had locked last night, was open. In a nightmare moment she saw them all in her imagination: robbers with skeleton keys, robbers with jemmies, robbers with sacks to carry away the swag; and each man wore a black mask and carried a deadly weapon—a bludgeon, a revolver, a dagger, a length of lead piping . . .

Gwen Kitson was recalled from her attackers by a painful sensation in her fingers: she was trembling so much that hot tea was slopping over the teacup into the saucer and scalding the hand that held it. She set the cup and saucer down on a hall chair, and, as she did so, she saw why the hall door remained open: it was wedged at the bottom by a pair of bedroom slippers—Tom's.

The imaginary burglars vanished. Tom must be responsible. She remembered that he had been found roaming out of bed one night when he had first come to stay with them. She remembered, too, the high words there had been then, with Alan, and she decided to manage this by herself.

First of all, she had a look outside on the landing: there was no sign of Tom. Then she removed the bedroom slippers, closed the door and went into Tom's bedroom. There he was, fast asleep—not even shamming, she was sure. She stood over him, the tell-tale slippers in her hand, wondering what she should say to him. She must scold him, and yet she did not want to be too hard on him and spoil his last day.

Even the mild reproach Aunt Gwen had prepared was never uttered. Tom, when she roused him, behaved in a way that too much alarmed her. He opened his eyes, but then at once squeezed them shut again, as if against a hateful sight. With his eyes closed, he began talking violently and in what seemed a senseless way: 'No! Not this Time! Not Now!'

Aunt Gwen dropped the slippers and fell on her knees by the bed, putting her arms round him. 'What is it, Tom? You're awake now. It's morning. You're safe and sound here with me.' He opened his eyes and stared at her and then around him, as though he had expected to see someone—and somewhere—else. 'Have you been in a nightmare, Tom? But, anyway, it's over. Why, here we are on Friday morning, and tomorrow you're going home!'

Tom did not answer her, but gradually the unnatural fixity of his look was broken. His aunt kissed him, and then slipped away to fetch him a fresh cup of tea. All she said to her husband was, 'It's time, for his own sake, that Tom went home. He's terribly strung up. Bad dreams —nightmares——' She thought of a new explanation of the bedroom slippers: 'I shouldn't be surprised if he even walked in his sleep.'

Aunt Gwen did not mention to Tom the bedroom slippers found in the doorway; and Tom, later observing them lying by his bed, only thought they were yet another part of the mystery of his being here at all. With him under the bedclothes—the laces twined round the fingers of his left hand—were Hatty's skates that had taken him to Ely; and yet here he was, on Friday morning, in the Kitsons' flat. He had felt so sure of being able to exchange his

Time for an Eternity of Hatty's, and he was back again after only a few hours of her existence.

'But perhaps that was because I let myself fall asleep, in the gig,' Tom thought, and resolved that such a thing should not occur again. For he still had another chance; he had tonight. Tonight he would go down to the garden, and stay there for as long as ever he pleased.

He debated whether to take the skates with him or not. If the great frost were continuing, he was willing to skate on the pond or on the meadow; but he was not willing to forgo the garden altogether as he had done last time.

Perhaps, anyway, the season in the garden would be summer, as it used to be . . .

Tonight, when he opened the garden door, the air that met him might be warm and soft and smelling of flowers. The yew-trees across the lawn would welcome him. He would go down the sundial path, and then turn right and run along the shadowy tunnel-path between the yew-trees and the nut stubs, and come out into the sunshine again by the asparagus beds, and perhaps see Abel digging a root of horse-radish by the early apple-tree and Hatty, a little girl again, in her blue pinafore, waiting to spin her tales for him.

'For Time in the garden can go back,' Tom reminded himself; 'and she may be a little girl again tonight, and we shall play games together.'

Friday was spent mostly in getting ready for Tom's going home. His things were collected and gone through; his suitcase was polished and re-labelled; and his aunt took him out shopping to choose what delicacies he would like for his packed lunch on the train and what little presents he would take with him to his mother and father and Peter. Tom could not feign interest in what seemed so far away in time. It might be years before he saw his home again tomorrow.

That night Aunt Gwen left both bedroom doors open so that she could hear Tom if he got out of bed in his sleep. Tom did not fail to notice his aunt's device. His midnight cunning and soundlessness had grown with weeks of practice: he was out of the flat and starting downstairs without having disturbed the sleepers.

He had seen from his bedroom window that the sky was overcast; there was neither moonlight nor starlight. As he went downstairs, he could hardly see the oblong of the landing window. 'It doesn't matter, though,' Tom said, and felt his way surely down the lower treads and so into the hall.

Here he stopped to listen to the grandfather clock, as though it might have some message for him; but the clock minded its own business, and its ticking only gave a measured reproof to him for the over-hasty beating of his heart.

He went down the hall, turned left at the old boot-cupboard, and was at the garden door. Suddenly he was in a panic to be out: he tore at the fastening of the door; and, though it was the wrong fastening that his fingers found, he would not allow himself to think of that.

'I'm going to get into the garden,' he said between his teeth; and the clock's ticking behind him neither confirmed nor contradicted his words.

He had got the door open now; and it was night outside,

too, as black as the night indoors. He could see nothing. He stood on the doorstep and sniffed the air. There was no frost in it, and yet there was no lingering summer perfume from shut flowers and from grass and leaves. The air seemed empty of smell, except for a faint tang that he could not quite place.

'It doesn't matter,' said Tom. The blackness did not matter either, because by now he knew the garden by heart. Blindfold, he could have found his way. Where should he go first? Across the lawn, to the yew-trees.

He sprang forward and began running. His bare feet fell on to cold stone; he knocked against a tall metal thing, and its lid fell off and rang upon stone again. He shied away, and still ran on in the direction of the yews, but long before he reached trees, crashed into a wooden fence, and knew that the tang he smelt had been of creosote, and that this was the creosoted fence enclosing the back-yard where the ginger-bearded man kept his car and where the tenants kept their dustbins.

He turned and ran then, like a rat with the dogs after it, back into the house. He could not have intended to make another attempt, for he did not close the garden door after him; he could not have intended to go back to bed, for he halted in the middle of the hall by the grandfather clock, sobbing. The grandfather clock ticked coldly on.

A light had gone on, somewhere along the landing up-stairs, and by it he could see a figure coming down the stairs. He knew in his heart that it could not be she, and yet he screamed to her for help: 'Hatty! Hatty!'

All over the big house, tenants were startled from their

sleep. Tom's call, sharp like a bird's warning, reached up even to the topmost flat and woke Mrs Bartholomew from a dream of her wedding one Midsummer Day some sixty-odd years before. The cry seemed to call her, and Mrs Bartholomew, muddle-headed with sleep like her tenants, put on the light and began to get out of bed.

Alan Kitson jumped the last few steps of the stairs and ran forward and caught Tom in his arms. The boy sobbed and fought as though he were being taken prisoner. Then his uncle felt his body go limp, and he began weeping softly now, but as though he would never stop.

Uncle Alan carried Tom upstairs, to where his aunt was waiting. Then he went down again to shut the garden door and to reassure the ground-floor tenants. Then he went up to his own floor and explained to the other tenant there that his wife's nephew had been sleep-walking. Finally, he mounted to Mrs Bartholomew's flat. He found her with the front door open, but on a chain. She was pale and trembling, and agitated by the crying she had heard. She listened to his explanation, but without seeming to believe or even to understand. She asked wilder and wilder questions, and asked the same ones again and again. At last, Alan Kitson lost patience with her, bade her an abrupt good night and hurried back to the flat below.

Aunt Gwen had got Tom back into bed and was giving him hot milk and aspirin. She came outside when she heard her husband in the hall. 'I shall stay with him until he sleeps,' she said in a low voice, 'for he seems quite ill with shock. I suppose it was his waking up and finding himself standing there, in the dark, all alone, not knowing he was in the hall—or, at least, not knowing how he got there.'

'Look,' said Uncle Alan, and held up a pair of old-fashioned skating-boots and skates. 'He was carrying these.'

Aunt Gwen was dumbfounded. 'What can have possessed him, even in sleep-walking?'

'And where can he have got them, that's what I'd like to know,' said Uncle Alan, examining them with curiosity. 'They've been oiled and polished recently, and yet they don't look as if they'd been used for fifty or a hundred years. I wonder . . .'

'You mustn't question him, Alan. Promise me that. He's not fit to be worried.'

'Very well. If they're his skates—and they're certainly not ours—I'd better put them with his things tomorrow, before he leaves.'

Aunt Gwen was going back into Tom's bedroom, but she remembered something that had puzzled her: 'When he called out, it sounded, from up here, as if he were calling someone.'

'He screamed for his mother, you mean, or his father?'

'No. Yet I thought it was *someone's* name.'

'It couldn't have been. He just screamed.'

XXVI

The Apology

SOMETIMES before in his life, Tom had gone to sleep in
disappointment or sadness, but always he had woken up
to a new day and a new hope. This time he found that the

morning was only a continuation of the night and the day before: even as his mind stirred awake, the horror and grief of yesterday were already there.

This was Saturday; he had lost his last chance; he had lost the garden. Today he went home.

The tears fell from his eyes, and he could not stop them falling. Aunt Gwen came to him early, and put her arm round him: 'But Tom, tell me—tell me what's the matter!'

Now, at last, he wanted to tell her—to share and perhaps thereby lessen his grief. But now it was too late: his story was too long and too fantastic for belief. He gazed at her in silence, and wept.

Tom had breakfast in bed, like an invalid. Over their own breakfast, the Kitsons discussed him.

'He really can't make that long train journey alone and in this state,' said Aunt Gwen. 'Couldn't we drive him home by car?'

Alan Kitson was perfectly willing. He worked on Saturday morning, so that they could not start until the afternoon. A telegram was sent to the Longs.

Tom got up and dressed very soon after his breakfast, because lying in bed and thinking was worse than being up could possibly be. He came out into the little hall just as his uncle was going off to work. His uncle and aunt told him of the change of plan, and Tom nodded.

Uncle Alan said good-bye and went out of the front door, and Aunt Gwen shut it after him. Almost immediately, however, she and Tom heard his voice in conversation outside, and in a few minutes he was back again,

P

looking annoyed. 'It's that old woman,' he said. 'Why can't she let well alone?'

'Mrs Bartholomew? What does she want now?'

'An apology for the disturbance last night. Of course, I gave her one at the time, and I apologized again just now; but she says the boy himself must go to her.'

'I shouldn't dream of sending him!' cried Aunt Gwen. 'It's outrageous of her to expect it! I shall tell her so!' Fully roused against Mrs Bartholomew, Tom's aunt made a move to the front door. Her husband stopped her.

'Careful, Gwen! She is the landlady. If we upset her, she could be very awkward.'

'All the same!'

'I'll try to soothe her myself,' said Uncle Alan.

'No,' Tom said suddenly, in a dull, steady voice: 'I'll go to her. I ought to. I don't mind.'

'I shan't let you, Tom!' cried Aunt Gwen.

'I shall go,' he repeated. It was like getting up instead of staying in bed, crying. You had to do these things—even unpleasant things: in a strange way, there was a relief in doing them.

There was something in Tom's manner that made his aunt and uncle respect his decision.

A little later that morning Tom climbed up to Mrs Bartholomew's flat and rang the front door bell. Mrs Bartholomew opened the door, and was face to face with him: she was as he had expected her to be—old and small and wrinkled, with white hair. All that he had not been prepared for were her eyes: they were black, and their blackness disturbed him—that, and the way they looked at him.

'Yes?' she said.

'I've come to say I'm sorry,' Tom began.

She interrupted him: 'Your name's Tom, isn't it? Your uncle mentioned it. What is your other name?'

'Long,' said Tom. 'I've come to apologize——

'Tom Long . . .' She had stretched out a hand and touched his arm with the tips of her fingers, pressing with them so that she might feel the fabric of his shirt and the flesh under the fabric and the bone beneath the flesh. 'You're real: a real, flesh-and-blood boy: the Kitsons' nephew . . . And in the middle of last night——'

Tom, trying not to be frightened by a queer old woman, said: 'I'm sorry about last night.'

'You screamed out in the middle of the night: you woke me.'

'I've said I'm sorry.'

'You called out,' she insisted. 'You called a name.' She lowered her voice; it sounded gentle, happy, loving—Tom could not say all the things it sounded, that he had never imagined for Mrs Bartholomew. 'Oh, Tom,' she was saying, 'don't you understand? You called me: I'm Hatty.'

The words of the little old woman were meaningless to Tom; only her black eyes compelled him. He allowed her to draw him inside her front door, murmuring to him softly and delightedly. He was in the tiny hall of her flat; and facing him was a Gothic barometer of familiar appearance.

'That's the barometer from the Melbournes' hall,' said Tom, as in a dream.

She was pushing him ahead of her into the sitting-room;

and facing him, from over the mantelpiece, was a large, brown, portrait-photograph of a young man with one of those ordinary faces that you yet remember and recognize again. Tom recognized this face: he had seen it last by moonlight.

'That's young Barty,' he said.

'Yes,' said Mrs Bartholomew: 'a likeness taken soon after we were married.'

With difficulty Tom's mind took in the meaning of what had been said: young Barty and the late Mr Bartholomew were one and the same.

He sat down heavily upon a chair, and faced her. 'You married young Barty? Who were you?'

'I've been telling you, Tom,' said Mrs Bartholomew patiently: 'I'm Hatty.'

'But Hatty was a girl when Queen Victoria reigned.'

'I'm a Victorian,' said Mrs Bartholomew. 'What is odd about that?'

'But Queen Victoria came to the throne in 1837.'

'That was a long time before I was born,' said Mrs Bartholomew. 'I was born towards the end of the Queen's reign. She was an old lady when I was a girl. I am a Late Victorian.'

'But I don't understand,' said Tom; 'I don't understand . . . The garden gone . . . and yet the barometer here . . . and you say you were Hatty . . . What happened after the day I skated to Ely with Hatty—the last time we saw each other?'

'The last time?' said Mrs Bartholomew. 'But, no, Tom, that wasn't the last time I saw you. Have you forgotten?'

She looked at him earnestly. 'I see you don't know all of our story, Tom: I must tell you.'

Tom listened as she began her tale; but at first he listened less to what she was saying than to the way she was saying it, and he studied closely her appearance and her movements. Her bright black eyes were certainly like Hatty's; and now he began to notice, again and again, a gesture, a tone of the voice, a way of laughing that reminded him of the little girl in the garden.

Quite early in Mrs Bartholomew's story, Tom suddenly leaned forward and whispered: 'You were Hatty—you *are* Hatty! You're really *Hatty*!' She only interrupted what she was saying to smile at him, and nod.

XXVII

A Tale for Tom Long

'IT was in the year 1895,' said Hatty Bartholomew, 'that
you and I, Tom, skated all the way to Ely: the year of
the famous great frost. That day, on the way home from
Ely, we met Barty, and he gave us a lift.'

She smiled. 'I'd never really talked to Barty before then,
for I was shy in company—I still am, Tom. But that day
was different: Barty and I were alone together, and we
talked, and we began to know each other. Barty used to
say afterwards that, before he had turned the gig into the
drive here, he'd as good as made up his mind that he
wanted me for his wife.

'So, some time later, he made me a proposal, and I

accepted him; and Aunt Melbourne was only too glad to get me off her hands.

'I was married on Midsummer Day, a year or so after the great frost; Midsummer Eve was the eve of my wedding day. Doing the last of my packing that night, I remembered my skates, and that made me remember you, Tom. I'd kept the skates where I'd promised you that I would, and I knew that I had to leave them there, although it was so long since I'd seen you. I wrote a note of explanation and left it with the skates.'

'I found it,' said Tom. 'Signed and dated.'

'Dated Midsummer Eve, in one of the last years of the old century. That Midsummer Eve was very hot, sultry and thundery. I couldn't sleep. I thought of my wedding the next day, and, for the first time, I thought of all I would be leaving behind me: my childhood and all the times I had spent in the garden—in the garden with you, Tom.

'There was a thunderstorm coming nearer, and there was lightning. I got out of bed and looked out of my window: I could see the meadow and the elm-tree and even the river-bank—I could see it all by the flashes of lightning.

'Then I thought I would look at the garden, by the same light; I had a great longing to see it. I went into an empty bedroom at the back of the house, overlooking the garden, a spare bedroom.'

'I think I know the one you mean,' said Tom. 'I stuck my head through the door, once.'

'Well, I stood at the window and looked over the garden. The storm was very close; the lightning flashes made everything very clear. I could see the yew-trees and the fir-tree and the greenhouse, as if by daylight. Then I saw you.'

'Me?' cried Tom. 'But I don't understand. When? I didn't see you.'

'You never looked up. I think you had been walking round the garden, for you appeared from one of those little corner paths and walked across the lawn to the house porch. You looked as thin through as a piece of moonshine. You were wearing your pyjamas—they were pyjamas, weren't they, Tom? In those days, most boys wore nightshirts, and I didn't know of pyjamas. Your pyjama jacket was flapping open, I remember.

'You reached the porch, and I suppose you went indoors, for that was the last I saw of you. I stayed on at the window. I said to myself: "He's gone; but the garden is here. The garden will always be here. It will never change."

'Do you remember the tall fir-tree, Tom—with ivy all the way up? I've stood under it many a time, as a child, when there was a high wind, and felt the earth heaving under my feet, as if the roots were pulling like muscles. That Midsummer Eve, when the storm was at its worst, and I was watching it, a great wind caught the fir and —oh, Tom, it was terrible to see!—the lightning struck it, and it fell.'

There was a deep silence, and Tom remembered the silence he had heard after the falling of that tree, and the cry from the upper window that he had heard in it.

'And then I knew, Tom, that the garden was changing

all the time, because nothing stands still, except in our memory.'

'And what happened next?' asked Tom.

'Oh, the next day, Abel complained of the fir-tree and that it had ruined one of his asparagus beds in its fall; but I forgot the fir-tree, and the garden, and you, too, Tom, because this was my wedding day. Barty and I were married and went to live on one of his father's farms in the Fens; and we were very happy.'

'And then?'

'Things went well for us—much better than they did for the cousins here. All three of them were in the family business to begin with. Then Hubert and Edgar went off, and James carried on alone. He married and raised a family; but his wife died, and the business went from bad to worse, and in the end he decided to emigrate. Before he went he sold everything—house, furniture and what land was left.

'Barty and I came over for the auction. The house already looked very different by then. James had been short of money, and so he'd sold first the two meadows, and then the orchard, and then even the garden. The garden had quite gone, and they were building houses at what had been the bottom of it, with their garden strips where the yew-trees and the lawn had been. None of the trees was left standing, except Tricksy. You can still see Tricksy standing in one of those gardens.'

Tom said, 'So that's Tricksy.'

'At the auction, Barty bought some of the furniture that I fancied—the barometer you saw, and the grandfather clock, that I'd always loved to hear striking. When I was a little girl, Tom, I used wilfully to misunderstand its hour sometimes, in the morning, and get out of bed and go downstairs before the maids—before sunrise, even—to play in my garden.'

'But you couldn't take the grandfather clock away with you into the Fens,' said Tom. 'It couldn't be moved.'

'It never needed to be moved,' said Mrs Bartholomew, 'for Barty bought the house—he would always buy anything I fancied, if he could; but he said it wasn't a gentleman's house any more, with no garden to it. He made flats out of it, and let them.'

'And then you came to live here?'

'Not then. Barty and I were very happy in the Fens. We had two children—boys. They were both killed in the Great War—the First World War they call it now.' Mrs Bartholomew did not cry, because she had done all her crying for that so long ago.

'Then, many years later, Barty died, and I was left quite alone. That was when I came here; and I've lived here ever since.'

Mrs Bartholomew stopped, as if that were the end of her story, but Tom prompted her. 'And since you've come to live here, you've often gone back in Time, haven't you?'

'Gone back in Time?'

'Gone back into the Past.'

'When you're my age, Tom, you live in the Past a great deal. You remember it; you dream of it.'

Tom nodded. He understood so much now: why the weather in the garden had always been perfect; why Time in the garden had sometimes jumped far ahead, and sometimes gone backwards. It had all depended upon what old Mrs Bartholomew had chosen to remember in her dreams.

Yet perhaps Mrs Bartholomew was not solely responsible for the garden's being there, night after night, these last weeks. For she remarked to Tom now that never before this summer had she dreamed of the garden so often, and never before this summer had she been able to remember so vividly what it had *felt* like to be the little Hatty—to be longing for someone to play with and for somewhere to play.

'But those were the things I wanted here, this summer,' said Tom, suddenly recognizing himself exactly in Mrs Bartholomew's description. He had longed for someone to play with and for somewhere to play; and that great longing, beating about unhappily in the big house, must have made its entry into Mrs Bartholomew's dreaming mind and had brought back to her the little Hatty of long ago. Mrs Bartholomew had gone back in Time to when she was a girl, wanting to play in the garden; and Tom had been able to go back with her, to that same garden.

'But these last few nights, before last night,' said Tom, 'you've hardly dreamt of the garden at all; you've been dreaming of winter and skating.'

'Yes,' said Mrs Bartholomew. 'Of skating to Ely—the farthest I'd ever been from home; of growing up, and of Barty; I dreamed less and less of the garden and of you, Tom.'

'I suppose you couldn't help that,' said Tom, 'if you were

growing up. I noticed, the night before last, in the gig, you talked to Barty all the time; never to me.'

'You were getting thinner—thinner through—every winter that I saw you,' said Mrs Bartholomew; 'and, by the end of that drive home with Barty, you seemed to have vanished away altogether.'

Tom said, without bitterness, 'And so, last night——'

'Last night I dreamt of my wedding day and of going away from here altogether, to live in the Fens.'

'And last night,' said Tom, 'when I went down and opened the garden door, the garden wasn't there any more. That was when I screamed out. I called to you, but I never really thought you could hear me.'

'You woke me,' said Mrs Bartholomew. 'I knew it was Tom calling to me for help, although I didn't understand, then. I couldn't believe you were real, until I saw you this morning.'

Tom said: 'We're both real; Then and Now. It's as the angel said: Time No Longer.'

From far downstairs in the hall came the sound of the grandfather clock striking. It struck two, and Mrs Bartholomew—who seemed to understand its language—said the hour must be eleven. Tom's aunt must be wondering where he was. Tom went downstairs to ask whether he might take a mid-morning cup of tea with Mrs Bartholomew. Aunt Gwen was too much surprised to object or even to question him.

He came back to Mrs Bartholomew, and she had just brewed the tea and brought out seedcake to eat with it. Over this, they settled down to talk of the garden.

They exchanged tales and secrets. Tom asked after Abel, and Mrs Bartholomew said that he had married Susan and they had had a large family and lived happily. Then Tom told her that Abel had been the only other person, besides herself, ever to see him. 'Fancy!' said Mrs Bartholomew, much struck. 'And Aunt Melbourne was always so scornful of Abel: she used to say he was as stupid as a cow in a meadow.'

'Well,' said Tom, warmly, 'the cows in the meadow could see me; and *she* never could.'

Mrs Bartholomew laughed at that—she could afford to laugh at Aunt Melbourne now; and then she, in her turn, told Tom a secret of the garden. She confessed to a disobedience of long ago. 'You told me not to carve marks and initials on the tree-trunks, Tom; but, when you'd taught me how to swarm Tricksy, I carved both our marks there: a long thin cat for you, Tom, wearing a hat for me—oh dear, it did look ridiculous! I never told you.'

'I once planned to climb the yard fence, to look at Tricksy,' said Tom. 'I wonder if I should have found the mark there.'

'It may still show.

So their talk of the garden rambled on, until the grandfather clock struck for noon, and Tom jumped up, for he must go. Lunch would be ready downstairs; and after lunch he was to be driven home.

'But you'll come again!' cried Mrs Bartholomew. 'And what about that brother of yours, that I saw in Ely—what was his name?'

'Peter,' said Tom, and started guiltily to think how he

had forgotten Peter, first of all in the horror of losing the garden, and then in the amazement and joy of finding it again in Mrs Bartholomew's remembrance.

He sat down again and told her about Peter, and especially of how Peter had loved to hear about the garden and of their adventures there. 'You must certainly bring him to visit me,' said Mrs Bartholomew, firmly. 'Will you be sure to tell Peter that I shall be expecting him?'

Tom promised. He found that, after all, he was looking forward eagerly to going home. There would be the warmth of that homecoming; and, when the welcomes were over, he would draw Peter aside into the little back-garden and whisper: 'Peter, I've the secret of the other garden to tell you, and I've an invitation for you from Hatty.'

Meanwhile, Tom must really say good-bye to Mrs Bartholomew now, or he would be late for lunch and for going home. Already Aunt Gwen was anxiously looking out for him, on the floor below. From the front door of Mrs Bartholomew's flat, Tom saw her on the watch; and Mrs Bartholomew saw her too.

'Good-bye, Mrs Bartholomew,' said Tom, shaking hands with stiff politeness; 'and thank you very much for having me.'

'I shall look forward to our meeting again,' said Mrs Bartholomew, equally primly.

Tom went slowly down the attic stairs. Then, at the bottom, he hesitated: he turned impulsively and ran up again—two at a time—to where Hatty Bartholomew still stood . . .

Afterwards, Aunt Gwen tried to describe to her husband that second parting between them. 'He ran up to her, and they hugged each other as if they had known each other for years and years, instead of only having met for the first time this morning. There was something else, too, Alan, although I know you'll say it sounds even more absurd... Of course, Mrs Bartholomew's such a shrunken little old woman, she's hardly bigger than Tom, anyway: but, you know, he put his arms right round her and he hugged her good-bye as if she were a little girl.'